SOMEBODY

TO

LOVE

Cover Artist: Natasha Snow Designs

Editing: Proof Positive

Proofreading: Judy's Proofreading

Formatting: Rainbow Danger Designs

Paperback: 978-1-9994727-8-8

Ebook: 978-1-9994727-9-5

So please just hold on to me
  This is no end, we're not finished here
  Finding our way, we're just changing

ONE

REMY

I INHALED DEEPLY, allowing smoke into my lungs for what would be the last time. The warm Palm Springs breeze felt cool against my skin, dampened from having been in the pool. This wasn't my house. I'd been staying with an older guy I met online after having been evicted from my lavish Los Angeles penthouse apartment over four months ago. My career—if you could call it that—had finally imploded once the world saw how truly fucked up I was. I hadn't had savings because I was a reckless fuck, and I'd found myself temporarily homeless.

I looked to my left at the setting sun, numb to the beauty of the colors lighting up the sky. Purples, blues, oranges, and pinks were on full display to be admired, yet all I saw was the end. The end of the day, the end of light, the end of everything I'd come to know. I sighed, then stubbed out the roach on the concrete roof I sat on. He didn't like it when I climbed up here—fuck him. He wouldn't have to deal with me after today. I looked to my right where the desert seemed to stretch on for miles—maybe forever. The thought filled me with a mix of dread and familiarity. If I went in that direction, I could tell myself I could run forever. I was used to running—it was the forever part that fucked me up and made me realize how little time I had left. I turned back toward the setting sun, laughing bitterly.

The sun had fully disappeared behind the mountains, taking some of its warmth with it. *Now is as good a time as any.* I stood, leaving the roach behind, and ran to the edge of the roof. My feet left the flat concrete and I felt weightless for a few gratifying seconds before gravity pulled me down. I hit the water feet first, sinking nearly to the bottom of the pool. If I could have stayed down there—away from all the noise —maybe I wouldn't have felt like I needed to reach the end.

Guilt ate at me over my selfishness and cowardice, but it wasn't a surprise that I was a fucking coward. I owed too many apologies to the people in my life, though one person stood leagues above the others. I'd wronged him the most. I'd hurt him when all he'd done was love me.

My lungs burned. I pushed against the bottom of the pool, surfacing on a gasp, then swam to the edge. Once I'd caught my breath, I hauled myself out of the pool, and headed toward the glass sliding doors. My phone rang, which struck me as odd. No one called me anymore—not after the truth had come out. Maybe it was morbid curiosity, or maybe just the last shred of hope I had in me, but I changed course and jogged toward my phone on one of the lounge chairs.

The caller ID showed a Chicago number, immediately setting me on edge. My sister was the only person in Chicago I still talked to, and I had her number programmed in my phone. I answered the call on what had to be the last ring, and gave a cautious greeting—I didn't need to be thinking about this random caller while I drifted off.

"Hello. I'm looking to speak with Remington Kincaid." The voice belonged to a woman. She sounded gravely serious, yet unaffected.

"You've got him."

"This is Northwestern Memorial Hospital. You were listed as the next of kin for Maxim Aver…" She trailed off before going on to butcher his last name.

"*Averkiyev*," I corrected, annoyance clear in my tone before I registered who was calling. "Is he okay?"

"Mr. Averkiyev was in an accident."

If she said anything after that, I didn't hear it. I dropped the phone, and bolted inside to get changed. All thoughts of the prescription drugs I'd planned on overdosing on were replaced with the gut-wrenching fear that Maxim was injured, or worse. That person I'd hurt the most—that was Maxim. I had to get to him and make sure he was all right—he had to be. I needed him to be.

I WENT straight to the hospital from the airport. I flew past the waiting area, heading for the nurses' station. Suddenly, a firm grip on my upper arm jerked me to a stop. My fist balled tight, and I was ready to lay into whoever had the audacity to grab me, though when I turned and saw who it was, all of the flight in me fled. I stood face-to-face with one of the few people in this city who knew how deplorable I was: Maxim's best friend, Mac fucking Buchanan.

His brown eyes narrowed on me, and his fingers squeezed harder before he let go. "What are you doing here?" he asked. There was no mistaking from his icy tone that he wasn't happy to see me. Then again, he and I never clicked, no matter how much Maxim wished we would get along.

I squared my shoulders and flexed my fingers around the strap of the overnight bag I'd flown across the country with. *None of your fucking business.* The words were ready to spill out, but I bit my tongue and swallowed them. "I'm here to see Maxim."

"Yeah, I figured as much, but why—are—*you*—*here*? It's been, what, almost eleven years, and you conveniently drop in when he's in the hospital?"

Just breathe. "A nurse called me. I'm still listed as his next of kin." The fight drained out of his face, replaced with utter shock. I'd have smiled and felt smug about it under other circumstances. I checked the nurses' station over my shoulder —they were busy talking to someone else. Seeing Maxim wasn't going to happen right away, I faced Mac again and tried to keep any traces of sass or condescension out of my tone. "Do you know what happened to him? I panicked when the nurse called, and didn't listen to the details."

He nodded. "He was on a jobsite a few blocks away. An apprentice didn't properly rig up some cables and was almost crushed by steel beams. Maxim was able to save him, though he fucked up his right shoulder. He's out of surgery, but they won't tell me more than that."

I exhaled deeply, feeling like I was breathing for the first time since my phone rang back in Palm Springs. "Thank fuck."

"Um, what?"

"He's alive," I clarified. "I was in such a hurry to get here, I hadn't stayed on the phone long enough to find out if he was even alive. I"—I looked over my shoulder and saw the nurse at the desk was free—"need to go. I'd like to get in and see him if he's stable."

"Can you tell him I'm here? A bunch of us are," he said, motioning to a group of men, and a blonde woman I vaguely recognized.

"I'll tell him when he wakes up."

The nurse closed the door to Maxim's room behind me. It was a shared room decorated in too much white and dated wall art. The other patient seemed to be asleep behind a half-drawn curtain. I approached Maxim's bed and drew the curtain closed behind me. His right arm was in a brace, and there was a fresh bandage on his shoulder. His face had a few minor scrapes, though none of them looked serious. They'd clearly been cleaned up, and didn't one bit take away from the fact that he was still the most handsome guy I'd ever seen.

I studied his face, searching for the changes a decade was sure to bring. For the most part, he looked the same. Where he'd been clean shaven before, he now had a few days' worth of stubble. The slightly curved scar on his upper lip was every bit as inviting as it'd always been. It was one of my favorite places to kiss him back when I had that right. His brown hair was shorter now, just a couple of inches on top and shorter on the sides. If it were any longer it would start to curl. He now had faint lines around the corners of his eyes and creases between his brows.

Those made me yearn for what I'd lost. I'd loved his expressions. What others thought was a scowl I knew to be a look of deep contemplation or worry. Maxim had always had the world on his mind, yet I'd been able to tell exactly what each of his expressions meant. His eyes moved behind closed lids, and a small rueful smile pulled at my lips. I sat down in the chair next to the bed and placed my hand on his.

"I used to love watching you sleep," I whispered, brushing my thumb over the rough skin of his hand. I leaned down and kissed his arm, then carefully rested my head on the bed next to his hand. The past six hours had been draining. Finally seeing Maxim alive and relatively okay had killed all of the adrenaline that'd been keeping me going.

Who knew what a difference six hours could make. I should have been dead, and in the bed of a man who essentially saw me as his property. Instead, Maxim's body heat bled into me as I drifted off to sleep, never happier to be alive.

TWO

MAXIM

I HATED TAKING DRUGS of any sort. I'd always had an awful tolerance, and they messed with my head—especially anything illicit or prescription strength. I remembered that I was in an accident on a jobsite, though everything was blurry after the ambulance arrived. Likely after they gave me drugs to manage my pain.

My eyes felt liked they'd been glued shut, and I didn't yet have the strength to open them. I could feel that my shoulder was in a sling or brace of some sort, though the pain was merely a dull throb. Clearly, I was still doped up. Having strong drugs in my system would also account for the strange dream I'd had. The bluest eyes I hadn't seen in years peered down at me, and the smoky voice I only knew from memories sounded clearer, closer. I'd definitely been dreaming.

An itch near my wounded shoulder got my attention. I tried to scratch it with my good arm, but I couldn't move it. It felt heavy, weighed down somehow. *Am I still asleep?* I wiggled my fingers, and they prickled with pins and needles —someone was definitely on my arm. My mind instantly went to Macalister. It wasn't at all shocking that my best friend would have found a way to sneak in, and he was a fairly tactile guy. He usually respected my wish for space, though if I were unconscious I could see how he'd seize that opportunity to sneak in a cuddle, or so he'd say. Yet, somehow, this didn't feel like him.

Despite the drugs, I was almost certain this wasn't Macalister. It didn't... feel right. He had scruff, and though the sensations in my arm were weakened, this felt like someone without a beard. Blake, perhaps? She wouldn't be far behind Macalister. I took a deep breath, stilling when a scent I hadn't noticed earlier came to my attention: chemicals. Specifically, the smell of a pool.

I tried again to open my eyes, but only managed to crack one lid. It was enough to see a wave of bleached hair so light that it was almost white. I forced myself to blink until I was able to get both eyes open. As the figure came into focus, I noticed dark roots growing in beneath hair that was more pale gray than stark white. His neck was lightly tanned and he wore a white T-shirt. A tattoo peeked out of the back of his shirt, something purple and black that I couldn't decipher. His face was out of view, yet something about him seemed so familiar. Then I saw it: a small scar on the upper cartilage of his left ear. It was from a cut I'd put there by accident.

A bitter laugh tried to escape me, but my throat was too dry. I must have still been dreaming. There was no way that Remy was *here*—he... why would he be? As if determined to obliterate my doubts, he sighed in his sleep, and I knew without a doubt that it was him. Before I could retreat inside myself and panic, a light knock sounded on the door, then a doctor entered.

He looked young—almost alarmingly so, with wavy brown hair that curled past his ears, blue eyes full of optimism, and a huge smile directed at me. He came to stand at my right side, checked his chart, and kept his voice low when he spoke. "Good morning, Mr. Aver... key... do you mind if I call you Maxim? I mean, I can totally try for your last name, but you'll have to forgive me for my poor pronunciation." His smile turned apologetic and he bit his bottom lip.

"Maxim is fine," I scraped out.

"Thank you. I'm Dr. Rey, and I'll be doing your rounds today. If you need anything at all or experience any pain, give that button there"—he indicated to the call button near the bed—"a push and I or a nurse will be over in a jiffy. Can I get you some juice or water?"

"Water, please."

He looked around, spotting a plastic cup of water on my nearby tray. He picked it up then frowned. "A nurse must have brought this earlier. All the ice has melted. Give me a minute and I'll grab more."

I shook my head, frowning at the slight pull on my shoulder. "It's okay." Dr. Rey nodded, then held the cup to my lips, slowly tipping it up. As strange as I felt having someone else feed me water, the relief to my throat more than made up for it.

Once the cup was empty, Dr. Rey returned it to the table before he turned his attention back to me. "All right, Maxim. It's question time. I've got some things I need to ask you, then I'm open to answering any questions you've got for me. Sound good?"

I nodded, and he went through what he had to ask, making note of my answers on my pain levels, my side effects, and how much I'd slept. It had been years since my last hospital visit, though I was sure it wasn't this pleasant the last time. The doctor was young and enthusiastic, but he was thorough and genuinely seemed to care about my comfort. He finished his questions, rewarding himself with an air high five, then asked me if there was anything I wanted to know.

"What kind of drugs did they give me?"

"Let's see." Dr. Rey checked my chart, tapping his finger along the edge of the clipboard. "You're on a drip for fifty milligrams of tramadol every four to six hours. You mentioned you were feeling kind of hazy; if that doesn't improve in a few hours, I can have you switched to hydromorphone. We want you to be as comfy as possible. You know, given everything that's happened."

"It's fine. I have a low tolerance for any drugs."

He nodded and hummed. "Unfortunately, I do need you on something for a couple more days. It's my job to keep you as close to pain-free as I can while you're here. The good news is that the damage to your shoulder isn't permanent, but it's going to hurt pretty badly for at least three weeks—especially if you forgo meds upon discharge. Depending on your pain levels, you'll likely be prescribed some tablets of tramadol, or maybe just some Tylenol Three. I do recommend you follow up with your home recovery treatment, but I can't make you." One corner of his mouth lifted in a sympathetic smile.

"Thank you."

Remy sighed again, catching Dr. Rey's attention. He pointed his pen at Remy and quirked an eyebrow. "Your dude has been here all night. Visiting hours kind of ended at nine last night, but he was out cold—you both were—so I made the executive decision to just leave him here."

My eyes flashed wide, and I couldn't help the flush that crept up my neck and cheeks. Unable to get away, I turned away from the doctor in a feeble attempt to hide. He snickered under his breath then gently patted my knee.

"It's all good. I'm not here to judge you. However, it is my duty to make sure his head isn't hurting your arm."

I turned my gaze down to the top of Remy's head and felt a small smile tug at my lips. I shook my head before I remembered to speak. "He's fine."

"Okie. I'll be on my way then. If you need anything else, don't hesitate to push the button."

I thanked him, and he left the room. I turned my attention back to Remy, who was still sound asleep. I couldn't try to convince myself he wasn't there; the doctor had seen him too. I'd find out the why and how when he woke up. Until then, I needed to touch him—just for that last bit of doubt to melt away. A large part of me never thought I'd see him again, and now there he was.

I reached for him, momentarily having forgotten about my wounded shoulder. Pain lanced through my arm and shoulder, and I jerked and winced as tears welled in my eyes. Remy shot up with wide, dazed eyes that settled on me. I bit my tongue to keep from saying something stupid or pathetic, and instead reached up with my good arm and stroked his cheek with my thumb. My breathing caught unexpectedly, and I was about to pull my hand back when Remy leaned into my touch. He gave me a shaky smile, then put his hand over mine, clasping his fingers around mine, before returning our joined hands to the bed.

I swallowed hard and blinked at him—and all of his tattoos. His tanned skin was covered in ink from what I could see, his neck, his chest, and his biceps. There was only one on his right forearm, I noticed. His blue eyes stood out against his dark eyebrows, and his lips still looked as soft as I remember them being. He still had the same beautiful face, though surrounded by the bleached hair and tattoos, he looked even more striking. The only real change to his face was a small silver hoop nose ring on the left. It suited the rest of his new look.

"Hey. It's been a long time." His voice was just as shaky as his smile.

"It has."

"The, ah, nurse called me last night. I'm still listed as

your next of kin." He scratched at the back of his neck, clearly as uncomfortable as I was. "I came as fast as I could. Are you…"—his eyes traveled over to my shoulder—"are you in any pain?"

I shook my head. My shoulder was the last thing I was thinking about.

"Good. That's good. Look, Maxim, I'm—"

The door opened, and Macalister rushed inside the room looking like death warmed up. He spotted my sleeping roommate and kept his voice down when he spoke. "Thank God you're okay. You're okay, right?"

I nodded and grinned at him. Remy cast his eyes down and his jaw ticked. The two of them never got along.

"Fucking ace. *Someone* was supposed to tell me when you woke up, yet he must have conveniently forgotten."

Remy stood up, his fist clenched at his side. "I'm going for a walk. I'll be back later, Max." Without sparing Macalister another look, Remy left the room, closing the door behind him.

"God, how is that guy still such a fucking dick after all these years?"

I hummed and tried to sit up higher. Macalister ended up helping. "I woke up first. Not long ago."

"You're still defending him, I see."

"It's not like that."

"Yeah—not convinced. I'm dropping this for now because you're all drugged up and almost died, but we are so revisiting this discussion, dude." I nodded, and he continued asking me how I felt and if I wanted anything. When I answered that I was fine and didn't need anything, he told me that all of our close friends and some of our baseball teammates were in the waiting room. They'd been waiting all night, so I had Mac bring them in in small groups to not disturb the other patient.

Bryan, Elijah, Dubhlainn, and Blake came in first. Seeing everyone was wonderful, even though Blake cried, and I wasn't comfortable being the center of attention. Elijah understood that more than the others, what with his anxiety. After they made sure I was all right, he tugged on Bryan's sleeve, suggesting they leave and let me catch up on my rest. Bryan nodded at his fiancé and dragged Blake out with them. Dubhlainn stood facing me in Macalister's embrace.

"I don't know what I'd have done if you'd died, Maxim. Mac would have driven me fuckin' mad, and I probably would've ended up killing him," Dubhlainn said with a smirk.

"Is having a morbid sense of humor an Irish thing? Or are you just being a dick to me?" Macalister asked.

I snorted a laugh over their exchange, though I was fairly certain Dubhlainn was teasing. It was too easy with a guy like Macalister.

"Don't worry your pretty little head about it, love." Dubhlainn angled his head up and met Macalister in a kiss, then turned his attention back to me. "I'll keep this guy out of your hair for a few hours. I can't promise anything beyond that."

"Thank you."

"Oh, come on. I'm allowed to worry," Macalister whined as he was dragged toward the door. They bid me a final farewell before they exited the room. The only sound that remained was the beeping from the machines. I tried to shift again and let out a groan when a jolt of pain shot through my shoulder. Feeling thoroughly defeated, I relaxed into the uncomfortable bed and waited for Remy to come back. Although I still didn't know what I'd say to him when he did.

If he did.

THREE

REMY

Maxim was kept in the hospital for three more days while his shoulder was monitored. On the second day, a physical therapist introduced herself and showed him a variety of exercises he'd need to keep up with to maintain a full range of motion in his shoulder. Failing to do so would likely result in stiffness, which would be painful. I sat back and quietly listened to every word the physical therapist said, knowing Maxim wouldn't retain all of the information with the painkillers in his system. All of it would be included in writing, but I felt better hearing it straight from a professional.

As soon as I'd heard that the injury would keep him off of work for four to six months, and he'd be in a sling for around six weeks, I'd made the decision to stay in Chicago to take care of him. I hadn't told him yet. I hadn't even explained why I was there at all. I'd like to say that his friends or staff kept getting in the way, but that would be a lie. I was scared to tell him; if he turned me away—which he had every right to do—I'd have nothing. Less than that. I'd *be* nothing.

I was fine with that a few days ago, though now I wanted to be there for Maxim. I'd failed him ten years ago because I was a fucking idiot. That fact still remained, but I could do this for him. My debt to Maxim could never be paid in full, even if I had a lifetime to try. I'd do the best I could until he recovered, then I'd have to leave him again—for good this time.

The American Express I'd "borrowed" from the man who'd essentially rented me had been cut off. I used the last fifty bucks in my wallet to keep myself fed during Maxim's stay. I slept in his room when the cute young doctor allowed it, and out in the waiting area when he didn't. By the third day I was more than ready to get Maxim home. His drugs had been dialed back and he was walking around more, which was a relief to see. His flow of visitors stayed consistent, and I kept my distance to avoid fighting with Mac. Stressing out Maxim or getting thrown out of the hospital wasn't my goal, so as much as I didn't like it, I waited. It also gave me an excuse to avoid the tough chat we needed to have.

No matter who he was talking to, I constantly felt the weight of Maxim's gaze on me. His brown eyes tracked my every movement, even if he tried to be discreet about it. I knew he wanted to talk to me, but he wouldn't until we had proper privacy. Maxim didn't like talking about tough shit on the best of days; doing so in a public place would be a nightmare for him. We'd have plenty of time to talk if he'd let me take care of him.

On the third day after his surgery, he was prepped for discharge. His cute doctor returned to let Maxim know about his medications and recommended doses. Maxim's roommate had been discharged the day before, and I saw this as my chance to broach the subject of me going home with him. The cute doctor finished up his questions and even managed to get Maxim to laugh before he headed for the door. He cast me a small grin and nodded toward Maxim before he left, and it occurred to me that the tension between us wasn't as subtle as I'd hoped it was. Of course it wasn't. I was acting sketchy as hell—not a lover, not a friend... not anything, yet ever present.

I took a deep breath before I got up and dragged my chair closer to Maxim's bed. He was sitting up, slowing rotating his good shoulder. I didn't even pretend not to ogle the way his muscles flexed when he moved. He was so much bigger from when I'd seen him last. Being so stagnant was probably killing him. I sat down in front of him with a huff and an awkward smile.

"What is it?"

"No small-talk bullshit—okay. I don't want you to take this the wrong way, but I'd like to look after you while you recover. I know you don't need it, and I'm probably the last person you want it from, but I'd like to help if you'll let me."

Maxim's brow furrowed. "Why would I take that the wrong way? I don't hate you, Remy. I'm glad you're staying."

I should have told him I wasn't planning on staying, and I knew I was an asshole for not being upfront about it. When he looked at me with hope in his eyes, I didn't have the heart to shit all over that. It would be worse down the road when I did leave, but in that moment I just couldn't tell him. He might not hate me yet, though I was sure he would.

"Remy," he said, snapping me from my drifting thoughts.

"Sorry, what?"

"I asked you if you had a place to stay."

"Not yet. I'm still working out my money situation." Vague, but I wasn't in the mood to get into the intricacies of my broke status.

"If you weren't planning on something else, you could stay with me. My apartment isn't huge or fancy, but it's more than we had before."

If it was possible for a look of panic and regret to erase words from existence, Maxim was doing a fantastic job of it. We used to live together in a shitty studio apartment when we were kids. My affluent parents didn't have a problem with me being gay, though they had a huge problem with me dating below my station. The Kincaids had old money and were a shipping and textile force back in the day. My father was an accountant now, though the family fortune was more than enough to ensure none of us had to work. He'd always stressed the importance of being a self-made man before being rewarded with the family's money. They'd cut me off when I didn't break up with Maxim, and that small apartment was all we could afford. It'd been enough for us.

I could probably crawl back to them and be alleviated of my money problems, but fuck that. Staying with Maxim held infinitely more appeal. And he'd never judge me. "If you're sure about it, I'll stay with you." *Nothing would make me happier.* "It'll make it easier to look out for you," I added, trying to make it sound like a logic-based decision. As if I'd ever made those.

Maxim gripped the mattress on either side of him and nodded. There was more he wanted to say, though I doubted he'd say much more today after the slip he'd just made. I used to be the only one he'd talk to. I didn't expect that to still be the case.

When we first met at a summer camp, he was the quietest, shyest eleven-year-old boy I'd ever met. He had no friends and was teased and tormented over the stupidest shit. He was already taller than them, though he never fought back. The scar on his upper lip was from a cleft lip surgery, and those little assholes bullied him over it. Since then, he'd always tried not to draw attention to himself. My brazen little ass had ignored that and adopted him as my new best friend. I'd fought kids twice my size who had even dared to look at him sideways.

It had taken two weeks before he'd said a word to me. After that, he spoke more and more, but only to me. I'd felt like the luckiest kid in the world because he'd chosen *me*; I had to be special. No one else had made me feel like that, so I clung to him as much as he did to me, and we were inseparable for the rest of the summer. We'd kept in touch via email and phone calls during the rest of the year, but those summers together were what I longed for most.

"I'll leave it to you to tell Mac. It's no secret that guy hates my fucking guts."

Maxim hummed and nodded, smirking at me.

"And don't tell him I called him Mac. It was a slip, and it won't happen again." Everyone except Maxim called him Mac, though Maxim was partial to using full names for everyone aside from me. I did it purely to piss the guy off.

I made myself scarce while Maxim delivered the news to Mac, using the time to freshen up in one of the bathrooms on the next floor. After several days without a shower, I was in a pretty grungy state. Mac was already gone when I returned. Maxim was in the middle of changing into fresh clothes Mac had likely brought for him. I felt like a leering pervert for watching, yet I didn't make any effort to rip my gaze from his exposed back. The white bandage against his tanned skin reminded me that I was there to help, not ogle.

"Let me help." I stepped around the bed and stood in front of Maxim, who gently nodded his head once. I carefully removed the sling, as the physical therapist had shown us, then fed each of his arms through the sleeves of the pullover sweater. He'd already changed into a pair of sweat-pants—thank fuck. I had a feeling it was going to take me a while to get accustomed to being around Maxim in various stages of undress, and then there was bathing—*clearly I haven't really thought this through.*

Whatever. I'd do whatever Maxim needed, and I'd deal with it. I filled Maxim's prescriptions in the pharmacy down-stairs before I ordered us a cab. Uber would have been cheaper, but I didn't have a working credit card anymore.

Maxim had insisted that his friends all leave so no one had to witness him being wheeled out of the hospital. He didn't protest in front of the nurse, though I could tell he felt on display in the wheelchair. Once we were in the backseat of the car and he'd given his address, he relaxed against me. He was still doped up to manage the pain, so he was tired and a bit foggy. I helped him out of the cab and into his apart-ment, taking him straight to bed. Then I noticed that this was a *one*-bedroom unit. The living room was large and uncluttered. That was probably where I'd help with his shoulder exercises in a few weeks. The bedroom wasn't overly big. A king-sized bed took up most of the space, along with one nightstand and a tall dresser. The wall across from the door had a big window, though the dark brown curtains were closed. There was a closet by the door, which looked decent enough.

I tucked Maxim into his bed and made sure his shoulder was cushioned with all the pillows I could find before I set out to snoop—for lack of a better word. The apartment was clean yet spartan. Maxim was never fond of frivolity, and this apartment clearly demonstrated that. When we lived together before, I'd done all of the decorating. The overall lack of décor would have normally driven me crazy, but now it had me smiling to myself. Maxim seemed to be the same person I'd known intimately, and that was comforting.

I was hungry but too drained to care. I found a blanket in the hall closet, took a glass of water to Maxim's bedside, and then stretched out on the black leather couch. Four days of exhaustion and shit sleep knocked me out within minutes, and I dreamt of a shy boy with the darkest brown eyes I'd ever seen.

FOUR

MAXIM

I WAS SURROUNDED BY PILLOWS, but otherwise alone in my bed, when I woke. The pain in my shoulder was searing and far more intense than anything I'd felt during my hospital stay. I turned on my bedside lamp with my good arm, taking notice of a glass of water and the white paper bag with my prescription drugs on the nightstand. I had no recollection of putting them there, so Remy must have—

Remy. Where was he? He wasn't in bed with me, so I figured he was on the couch or had gone out. My head still felt a bit foggy, though I was much more lucid than I'd been in the hospital. I hadn't been thinking clearly when I suggested Remy stay with me. While I wouldn't mind sharing my bed with him, it hadn't occurred to me that he wouldn't want to. It was foolish of me to overlook telling him I only had a one-bedroom apartment. I mainly had the drugs to blame for my oversight, and I hoped I hadn't made things more awkward between us.

At the hospital Remy had acted like nothing was wrong —we both had. I wanted to believe that everything would be all right—that he'd finally come back for me—though I knew better than to get my hopes up. Remy never did anything with a specific reason. He didn't always explain himself, but he always had some sort of self-justification. I didn't believe him entirely when he said he'd come back to take care of me. I could tell there was something else, but I didn't have the energy to pry it out of him. It would come out in time.

I sat up, and immediately regretted that decision when it jarred my shoulder. I gritted my teeth and hissed through the pain, though it got better once I was leaning against the headboard. Not much, but enough that I could breathe without wincing. It was going to be a long few weeks without pain management, though it was better than living in a daze.

I got up, used the bathroom and brushed my teeth, then found Remy asleep on the couch. His lips were slightly parted, and his bleached hair was messily lying across his forehead. It looked so soft, and before I knew what I was doing, my fingers were brushing it back from his face. He looked like his twenty-year-old self—like the guy who'd left me—while he slept. I swallowed hard, then pulled his blanket up higher around his shoulders before heading for the kitchen. I didn't have much food: onions, carrots, condiments, and some chicken and veggies in the freezer. Although it was enough to make one of Remy's old favorites: chicken fried rice. Chopping onions and chicken with one hand was going to be a pain, but I had to figure out how to take care of myself. Remy was here now, but I knew that could change at any moment—just as it had before.

Remy woke up while I was frying the rice, chicken, and vegetables. It was pretty loud, and I felt sorry about waking him, though I was happy to see him standing in the entry to the kitchen, grinning at me.

"Is that chicken fried rice?"

I nodded at him, biting back a dopey smile.

He stepped closer and peered into the frying pan with a full smile. "You remembered."

I nodded again and scooped up one of the carrots I'd cut into stars—just the way he used to like them. I held the fork out for him to take, but he leaned forward and took the carrot with his teeth while I held it. My eyes were practically glued to his mouth while he chewed, then his throat while he swallowed. His Adam's apple bobbed beneath the tattoo on his neck. It looked like a raven or crow, though instead of a mass of heavy black ink, there was a lot of negative space and purple highlights. The wings spread out up under his jaw on both sides, yet it didn't look harsh, if that was the right word. It was a beautifully designed piece that I wanted to trace with my fingertips. Then again, I wanted to touch every inch of him.

A flush colored the negative space between the dark lines, and I looked up to see his cheeks were pink as well and his eyes were looking off to the side. Shit—I'd been caught staring. I stirred the rice one more time, then shut the burner off. My movements were already awkward with my left hand —having Remy in close proximity made me even clumsier. When reaching for bowls in the cupboard, I almost knocked over the whole stack, and then I managed to whack my good arm into the side of the fridge.

"Easy, big guy." Remy took my hand in both of his and rubbed my knuckles. "I'm supposed to be doing this anyway. Go sit down."

I retreated to the living room, and Remy brought food and drinks out moments later. He sat at the other end of the couch after hesitating, glancing between the couch and the matching chair. I watched out of the corner of my eye as he took his first bite. He hummed in satisfaction and leaned back into the cushions. "This is so good. I haven't had it in ages."

"You don't still eat it all the time?"

He shook his head, chewing another bite. "It never turned out the same as when you made it, so I stopped trying years ago."

I didn't know what to do with that, so I didn't say anything. The quiet never bothered me, though I was painfully aware of it with Remy next to me. For his benefit more than mine, I turned on the TV then passed him the remote. He put on reruns of *Arrested Development*, which was always one of his favorites.

We made it halfway into the first episode without exchanging another word. It wasn't at all like the comfortable, companionable silence we used to share. This was the result of avoiding the inevitable conversations we needed to have. I couldn't have Remy, or anyone, tiptoeing around me —it just wasn't going to work.

I took a deep breath to steel myself, then turned toward him, ignoring the pull in my shoulder. "Why did you leave?"

I didn't have to specify when I was referring to; he knew. His body froze mid-inhale for a few moments before he licked his lips and his breathing resumed. "Maxim, I don't think—"

"Please," I pleaded. "If I did something wrong, please tell me."

"It wasn't anything like that. You didn't do anything wrong." He turned away and his jaw clenched a few times. "I know I owe you an explanation, but I can't talk about that right now. I know that's selfish of me, so you don't have to tell me. Just... please understand that it wasn't because of anything you did or didn't do."

That wasn't exactly the answer I'd been hoping for, but I wouldn't ever force Remy to do anything he didn't want to do. Trying to control a guy like him was a fruitless endeavor and always had been. If he didn't want to do something, he wouldn't—not even to keep up appearances. Especially not for appearances. It drove his parents crazy when we were teens.

"I'm sorry I asked."

He huffed, then faced me again. "Don't apologize. I'm the asshole here." I didn't dispute that, though I also didn't think it was entirely true either. "I'll try to answer anything else you want to ask me."

"If I hadn't been injured, would you have ever come back?"

"Fuck me," he muttered. "I wanted to, but I don't think I would have." He must have seen the unspoken question in my eyes and continued. "I didn't think I could bring myself to. What could I have said to you to explain why I'd been gone so long? I still don't fucking know what to say."

"Why come back now?"

He rubbed the back of his neck, revealing another tattoo on his underarm—some sort of serpent, maybe. "I was in a bad place when the hospital called. When I heard you were hurt, or worse, I needed to get here. Nothing else was more important than seeing that you were all right."

"You still care about me." It wasn't a question, and I hadn't meant to say it out loud.

Remy's face contorted, and he almost looked offended. "Of course I still fucking care. I never stopped loving you, Max." He said my name so softly that I would have missed it if I hadn't been watching his lips.

Love. I sucked in a sharp breath, then nodded. I still loved Remy, though I was sure when he said it, he didn't mean he was still *in* love like I was. I'd tried to hate him. I tried for months, but I couldn't. Even when I'd given up all hope that he was coming back, I still loved him.

"You don't have to reply to that," Remy said, interrupting my thoughts. "I'm not trying to score any sympathy points. I know I did a terrible thing to you by leaving, and I'm not trying to soften that."

I needed to change the topic before I said something stupid. I couldn't trust myself to not tell him how pathetic I'd been, hoping he would one day come back to me. I took a drink of the water Remy had brought out, then cleared my throat for good measure. "Where have you been living?"

"New York at first. I've been in LA for the last eight years or so, though."

One corner of my mouth quirked. "That explains your tan. It's subtle, but you're definitely darker."

He snorted a laugh. "Yeah, all the SPF sixty sunscreen in California can only keep me so protected."

"What do you do out there?"

The joy in his eyes from a moment ago died, and I instantly regretted the question. "Not very much, if I'm being completely honest." I cocked my head in confusion, and he went on. "When I left Chicago, I didn't have any money. I stayed with friends and lived off my savings for a few years. I had enough to last two decades or more, though the company I kept enjoyed a fairly lavish lifestyle, and I pissed it all away. Well, I drank it and snorted it if you want me to be specific."

Remy had dabbled in cocaine when he was fifteen. We started dating a year later, and I got him to quit before it became a serious problem. It saddened me that he'd picked it up again, but I wasn't going to judge him. I nodded for him to continue.

"Instagram was starting to get really popular then, and my account garnered a bunch of attention because of who I was always seen with, and where. I got my first paid sponsorship in 2013, and it kept building from there. The more followers I got, the more companies contacted me."

"You've been able to sustain yourself doing that?"

He hummed. "With almost two million followers, I was able to charge one hundred grand per post on average. Once I became an"—he held up his fingers and made air quotes —" 'Internet celebrity' I also got large sums of cash for going to certain clubs. Being seen and photographed there, drinking specific brands of alcohol—shit like that."

I opened my mouth, then snapped it shut. I didn't know what to say. I knew people like that existed, but I never thought I'd know one. It seemed so absurd as a concept to me, yet at the same time I understood why people would be drawn to Remy and that kind of lifestyle. He was effortlessly charismatic, enough that even I'd been pulled in. I was pretty sure that was part of why he and Macalister didn't get along —they were too similar, though they'd never admit it.

"Unless I imagined it, at the hospital you said that money was an issue."

"Yeah. I haven't had a sponsor in a while, so things are pretty tight. My rent in LA is ridiculous." He flashed me a quick smile that didn't reach his eyes. I knew there was more to it. He'd tell me in time.

"Will staying here be problematic for you?"

"Not at all. The great thing about being Internet famous is that I can be anywhere." His tone was self-deprecating, which was new for Remy. "Besides, I already told you that there's nowhere I'd rather be right now."

"Okay. You don't have to worry about money while you're here. I have to meet with my supervisor at some point to fill out some paperwork, but I'm going to receive compensation since I was injured on the job."

Remy shook his head. "I didn't come here to mooch off of you."

"You won't be. Your money won't help me when I need someone to help me with tying my shoes, or any other simple task that will cause me trouble." I smiled at him to show I was being sincere.

"Hopefully I can be more useful than that," he said flatly. "While I appreciate that you made my favorite, you shouldn't have even cooked today. I should be doing that for you."

I snorted a laugh, wincing at the slight movement in my shoulder. "I can still cook sometimes, Remy. I'm not an invalid."

Remy bit his lip and nodded. "No, I suppose you're not. I mean it, though. I want to be useful, and I'll do whatever you need."

"Will you consider sleeping in the bed with me?" Remy's eyes widened, and I quickly elaborated. "I don't mean to imply anything by that. The couch isn't too comfortable for sleeping, and the bed is huge." My skin heated the more I spoke, and I wanted to hide. "You don't have to if you don't want to. I know it's kind of... weird."

"No, I'd like that. No offense, but your couch is lumpy as fuck." He flashed me a playful smirk, and we watched a few more episodes. This time the silence wasn't heavy. We still had a lot to discuss, but we'd made enough progress for one day.

THE REST of the day was much of the same, with Remy and me watching TV. We dropped the heavy subjects and stuck to safe, neutral topics. Remy told me more about what being an influencer was like, and how much he loathed that term. He asked me about my duties being an ironworker, which sounded dreadfully dull after the lavish stories he'd told me.

Even so, he paid careful attention to everything I said and asked me questions about the job.

My shoulder ached the entire time, worsening as day turned to night. I thought I'd done a fairly good job of masking how much it hurt, but I couldn't keep up the façade after supper. Sweat had begun to bead on my forehead while we were watching a movie and my breathing wasn't as steady as I tried to make it.

"Maxim, how bad is your pain right now?"

I shrugged, which was a mistake. Pain shot through my entire arm and up my neck, making my jaw clench and my eyes water.

"Dammit, why didn't you say something?" Remy shot up and headed down the hall. He returned a few moments later with my unopened bag of prescription drugs. He stood before me with a pained look that almost rivaled mine. "Why didn't you take your dose when you woke up?"

"I can't think straight when I take those."

Remy sighed and sat down on the armrest of the couch. He rubbed my good shoulder, while his fingers absently tapped on the closed paper bag sitting in his lap. "I'm not going to force you to take these, even if I think you should. You don't have to take the full dose if they mess with you too much. We can try half and see if that helps at all."

I shook my head gently. "I'm okay. I think I should go back to bed, though." I tried to stand, and I stumbled, dizzy from the pain. Remy caught me and helped me to my bed.

"Maybe tomorrow morning you can try a shower. I bet you're dying for one."

"Are you trying to tell me something?"

Remy snorted and shook his head. "Don't be a dick. You know I wasn't implying anything."

Laughter rolled through me, which I tried to stifle. I wasn't successful. Remy pouted as he aggressively fluffed up my pillows, though he was careful when he placed one under my arm. He pulled up the blankets, then sat on the edge on the bed with his hand on my chest. His hand on me served as a distraction from the throb in my shoulder, and one I welcomed. "Are you coming to bed?"

"Soon. I'd love a proper shower first. And a shave too." He scratched at his stubble and scrunched up his face.

"Help yourself to whatever you can find."

Remy asked me if I needed anything before he turned off the light and left the room. I heard the shower spray a minute later and tried not to think about all the showers we used to take together. I had to stop having those types of thoughts if I wanted to survive the next few weeks. My sling had to stay on for at least four weeks. If Remy was going to stay that long, I couldn't let my mind wander to the past every time I was reminded of the way things used to be. I had to accept that both of us had changed. He wasn't mine any longer, though in my heart I knew I always would be his.

I must have dozed off while I was waiting for Remy. My shoulder woke me after I tried to turn toward the warmth resonating from the other side of the bed. I sat up to take some pressure off of the back of my shoulder, which was on fire. Once the main burst of pain trailed off, I felt around in the dark until my fingers connected with warm, smooth skin. I lightly traced it until I reached Remy's collarbone. He was facing me, and still asleep from the sound of his breathing. I noticed at the hospital that he was every bit the heavy sleeper he'd always been, and I was glad for it. He had to be tired, and I'd hate to wake him needlessly. I withdrew my hand, then lay back down, wishing there weren't eleven years of distance between us. Wishing that I'd finally woken from the nightmare of a life without him.

FIVE

REMY

I THOUGHT I WAS STILL DREAMING when I woke up with Maxim next to me. He was turned on his side, facing away from me, giving me a nice glimpse of his T-shirt stretched over his broad shoulders. It would have been even better with the light on, but I wasn't about to complain. Being with Maxim had always felt so right—like our bodies were made for each other. I wondered if that were still true. Aside from my hair and tattoos, I hadn't changed too much physically since we were together last. Maxim on the other hand was broader, thicker, and it was probably my imagination, but he seemed taller than the six foot three he was before. A shiver ran up my spine at the thought of being with him now. Was he still tender and attentive? I'd bet he was.

I'd always had to push his buttons to get him to be rough with me. It was one of my favorite games to play, usually starting in the morning and building throughout the day. By the time we'd go to bed, Maxim would be so riled up and frustrated with me, and he'd work all of that out on my lucky ass. *What I'd give to feel you again*. I reached for him, then balled my fist and pulled it back before my fingertips made contact. I couldn't go fucking things up on the very first night. I wasn't there to fulfill my fantasies or relive moments passed. With that thought in mind, I carefully slid out of bed, went to the washroom, then cleaned up the mess I'd made in the kitchen the night before.

I needed to learn some new recipes if this cooking thing was going to work out. Maxim had always cooked for us before, but it was on me now, and I had a feeling ramen and boxed dinners wouldn't cut it for much longer. Given his physical fitness, I assumed he ate a lot of protein and veggies —healthy shit I never cooked for myself. I set myself a reminder in my phone to look up some easy, healthy meals, and I'd ask Maxim what he normally ate once he woke up. The state of his fridge was almost as grim as mine had been back when I had my own place, so we needed to grab groceries soon.

Until then, I found some oats, honey, and brown sugar, and Googled how to make oatmeal for breakfast. I brought it in for Maxim and was surprised to see him sitting up. "Good morning," I greeted, my voice tight at the sight of his stiff shoulders. He was in pain.

"Good morning."

"I made some breakfast. It's more carbs—sorry about that." I handed Maxim the bowl then stepped back and fiddled with my hands as he took the first bite. He made a face that wasn't quite enjoyment, yet not quite revulsion. "Oh, fuck, is it bad? I tried to follow the recipe."

Maxim shook his head while he took a drink of water. "It's not bad. It's just, um… sweet." He continued eating, dodging me when I tried to take the bowl back. I insisted that he didn't have to eat it if he didn't like it, but he wouldn't surrender it. "I don't dislike it, Remy. It's sweet because you've always had a sweet tooth. It reminds of those cookies you baked for my fifteenth birthday," he said with a smile.

I groaned. "Can we not think about those? I was high as fuck and forgot I'd already added the sugar."

"You forgot twice, love." His mouth snapped shut as soon as the words left it, and pleading dark brown eyes met mine. "I'm sorry about that." He sounded so fucking sad, and that shattered my heart.

"It's okay—really. It's like you said last night: we're in a kind of weird place, uniquely so. Hiccups are going to happen, and I'm sure it'll be awkward at times, but it's okay." I gave him my best smile and felt a wave of relief when he nodded. "Now, how about we figure out this shower situation?"

Figuring out the shower situation was far less exciting than I'd hoped it would be. We decided it was best to leave the sling on since the wound was still fresh, so I taped a bag around it to keep it dry. Since he wasn't taking his drugs, Maxim was steady on his feet and didn't need any assistance beyond the taping.

We went to get groceries after his shower. I'd offered to go solo so he could rest, but he had insisted on coming. It was a clear day, and the sidewalks were free of ice and snow, so I didn't see the harm. I only had T-shirts with me and had to borrow one of Maxim's sweaters. He tried to offer me his coat, but I declined and made him wear it. The sweater was perfect, anyway. It smelled just like him and was loose on me in that cozy, *curl up on the couch and relax* kind of way.

The walk there and back showed me that I not only needed a proper winter coat, but boots as well. Sneakers weren't sufficient, even for a mild Chicago winter day after coming from Cali. I was half frozen by the time we returned with as many bags of groceries as I could carry. Maxim had offered to carry some, and I'd turned him down for obvious reasons.

The remainder of the day was very much like yesterday. We sat and watched Netflix, interspersed with periods of light conversation. I tried to keep the topic off of me, but Maxim was far too interested in how I'd been living and kept steering the conversation back to me. As much as withholding the whole truth from him made me feel awful, telling him everything would be worse. I didn't want Maxim to pity me, or worse, be disappointed or disgusted. No matter what spin or disguised word was used to lessen the intent, I was a whore in every sense of the word.

I'd been a fame-whore for years, selling myself to the highest bidders for social media ads. After my "career" imploded, I stooped to a whole new low when I accepted an offer to be a live-in rentboy. It was that or porn, and my face was too recognizable for the latter. What else could a guy with literally no qualifications do?

I didn't go to university like Maxim did—I'd barely even graduated from high school. Without my family's name behind me, I was pretty fucking sure I'd have been expelled. At thirty-two, I almost considered myself lucky that someone would want to essentially be my sugar daddy—and wasn't that just fucked up? Had I been younger I could have charged more, though the money was still decent. That type of lifestyle had an expiration date, and I hadn't planned on being around to reach it.

As I prepared a simple dinner of roasted veggies and pan-fried steak in the cast iron skillet—apparently that mattered —I tried not to think of what I was doing as lying to Maxim. Those unnecessary details wouldn't help him get better any faster, so what was the point? It wasn't exactly something I wanted to advertise, either.

THE PAIN in Maxim's shoulder kept getting worse. For the better part of a week it'd kept him up at night, which meant I was up too. He tried to pretend he was sleeping, though I could tell the difference. Lying was always my game, not his.

I felt helpless watching him in pain day after day. While we were having supper a few hours ago, I tried to convince him to take his pills, though I knew he wouldn't—and he didn't. Things had been awkward after that, and Maxim didn't say another word to me other than his thanks for me cooking and a good night when we got in bed. I knew he was caught up in his thoughts, and trying to deal with the pain, so I tried not to take his silence as a punishment.

When his harsh breathing gave way to a whimper, I reached my limit. "Enough." I pushed the blankets off, then rolled out of bed, headed straight for Maxim's pills. I turned on the light and tore into the paper bag with his pills.

Maxim sat up with a wince. "Remy, what are you—"

"No." I found the right bottle and shook two tablets into my palm. "I can't lie there while you're suffering needlessly. Take the pills. I'll look after you." He shook his head and looked away, but I caught his chin and turned him back toward me. There was real fear in his eyes, and it broke my heart when I remembered why.

The first time I'd convinced him to come to one of my parties in high school, some asshole had roofied him. I found him before things escalated too far and had locked us both in my room for the rest of the night. When he'd woken up the next morning, he had no recollection of being drugged and escorted to one of the guest rooms. I had the awful burden of relaying what I knew had happened, and God, I wished I didn't have to tell him. I could have told him he'd drunk too much too fast, and he'd have believed me. But I'd told him the truth, and it terrified him. His memory of that night never returned, which I thought only made it worse for him.

I softened my approach and stroked my thumb along his jaw. "Do you still trust me at all?"

His brow furrowed, but he nodded. "Yes."

"Then please take the pills, Max. I know you're scared of not being in control, and I understand why. You can trust me to keep you safe just like I used to." I waited with bated breath, unsure of what I'd do if he said no again. Relief washed through me when he took the pills from my hand. That sad, scared look was still clear on his face, but he trusted me anyway. He tossed the pills back, and I brought the glass of water to his lips. When I set the glass down, I wanted to kiss his dampened lips and tell him everything would be all right—whether I believed it or not. Instead, I motioned for him to scoot over, and crawled in bed next to him. I held my arm out for him and then carefully pulled him into an embrace, shielding him. Protecting him.

THE NEXT FEW days were an improvement from a pain perspective, though Maxim was definitely out of sorts as a side effect. He wasn't steady enough on his feet to shower alone, which we discovered only after he'd almost wiped out. I'd tried to help him while staying out of the enclosed shower, which ended in a soaking wet disaster. The shower-head wasn't one of those ones you could extend, so it made the experience a hell of a lot harder than it needed to be. The next day, I'd gotten in with him, though I left my boxers on in hopes they would help remind me that I was there to *help* him, and nothing else.

I stayed close to him as much as I could, especially during the hours when the medication affected him most. He didn't have to ask me—and he never would—because I already knew. Drowsiness was another side effect that hit Maxim hard. The hours he spent asleep were utterly boring for me, though I was glad he was finally able to get more rest. I was staring at the blank TV screen when a knock at the door surprised me and made me jump.

I checked the peephole and banged my head against the door with a groan after I saw Mr. Blond Ambition himself on the other side of the door.

"I know you're in there," Mac said from the hall. "My knocks are only going to get progressively louder and more obnoxious until you open up, dude."

Knowing Maxim would want me to, I opened the door, then went back to the couch and sat down, leaving it up to him whether or not he followed me. Unfortunately he did.

"Where's Maxim?"

I nodded toward the hall, not taking my eyes off of the black TV screen. "Asleep."

"Has he been asleep for the last week and a half? I've been trying to reach him." His hands were on his hips and he had this indignant look on his face. His entire existence annoyed me.

"Gee, I don't know, it's almost like he's recovering from surgery or something."

"Dick," he muttered.

"Douche." I crossed my arms over my chest and looked away from him. We stayed locked in silence, as if it were a competition that I had no intention of losing.

"God, you're the worst," Mac finally said.

"Should I pass a message on for you, or something?"

Mac came closer to the couch and dropped down next to me, which struck me as odd. "Drop the attitude, Remington Steele." I cringed but didn't interrupt him. "How has he been?"

"In pain. He wouldn't take his meds for the first few days."

"And he is now?"

"Yeah. They make him tired, hence the"—I checked the time on my phone—"eleven o'clock nap. Shouldn't you be at work?"

He shrugged. "I work from home. Don't change the subject. How did you get him to take the pills?"

"I asked him to trust me."

Mac sighed, then shook his head. "Of course he still trusts you," he muttered. "I should have guessed that. You were always his weakness." He grinned at me, though there was no joy in the expression. "I don't know why you're really here, and frankly I don't care. All that matters to me is that you don't fuck with Maxim. He's too good for your bullshit, and I won't see you hurt him again."

"Is this the part where you tell me you'll kill me if I break his heart?"

"Not at all. I won't kill you, but I will break your nose." He stood up and walked around the couch toward the door. "He deserves better than you."

I chewed on the inside of my cheek until I tasted iron, then swallowed it down. "I know he does. I'm not here to fuck with him, or start things back up."

"Then why come back at all?" he asked, his brow furrowed.

I stood up and looked him in the eye when I spoke. "I'm selfish, and I wanted to see him again."

"That's it, huh?"

I shrugged and squared my shoulders. "It's the Spark-Notes version."

He snorted. "SparkNotes—you would. Please tell Maxim I stopped by. And to check his damn phone so I know he's alive." He opened the door, then stepped out, and I followed to the threshold.

"I'll pass it on. Goodbye, Macalister," I replied as I closed the door in the middle of him cursing me blue. I leaned against the door and listened to his angry footsteps fading down the hall. As much as I disliked that guy, I was grateful Maxim had him. Mac had been there for him when I wasn't, and I could never truly hate him because of it.

When Maxim came down the hall about an hour later, I was so lost in my thoughts that I didn't notice him until the couch dipped next to me. I was caught up in a moment from a lifetime ago when I'd made the worst decision of my life, then followed it up with the hardest. In one night, I'd destroyed my life with Maxim because I was weak and careless.

"Are you okay? You look upset."

I nodded and put on my best smile. "Yeah, I'm good. Mac dropped by a little bit ago."

"That explains why you're upset."

"Nah, it was fine. He was checking in on you. Apparently you haven't been adequately meeting Ken Doll's demands for communication."

Maxim huffed a laugh, then leaned back into the couch. "Dubhlainn told me to ignore him while I recuperated. He said he'd keep Macalister at bay for as long as he could."

"Who is that? Dove... what did you say?"

"Dubhlainn. It's an Irish name. He's Macalister's boyfriend."

I narrowed my eyes at Maxim while the words tried to penetrate. "Um, excuse me?" Maxim sighed at me and rolled his eyes. I understood clear enough it was him saying something along the lines of "you heard me—don't be immature." "You'll have to give me a minute with this. Since when?"

"Probably forever. He only realized it when he met Dubhlainn."

"Fucking hell. I knew that bastard wasn't straight. He played up the slutty jock way too much."

Maxim chuckled and bumped his knee into mine. "Calm down, Remy. Bisexuality exists, you know."

"Ugh, he would."

"Remy," Maxim warned.

"It's not everyone, it's just him."

"Yes, love." He closed his eyes and started to drift again. He must have taken a dose before he came out. Had he been conscious and lucid, he'd have noticed the slip, but I didn't mind. Maxim used to call me love more than anything, and it felt good to hear it again, even if it was only because of the drugs. It made me feel like I was still his and that I hadn't fucked everything up. The fantasy was superficial at best. Nothing could erase the emptiness I felt from being away from the guy I loved most for so long, and worse, knowing it had been the result of my own actions.

I wasn't that same person anymore—I was worse. Lower morals, lower standards, and no integrity. My love for Maxim and my self-loathing were the only things to remain unchanged over the years. My shallow life had nothing to do with my environment, and everything to do with my heart being left behind, along with a smooth, gold band that once served as a promise—a promise I'd broken before I ever even had the chance to officially make it.

Mac didn't know just how spot-on he was; I truly was the worst.

SIX

MAXIM

I T TURNED OUT THAT MACALISTER wasn't the only person who'd been trying to reach me. When I finally checked my phone, I had several concerned voicemails from my supervisor. I'd completely forgotten to call him and let him know I was all right. One of the guys on my crew must have filled him in because he had details about the accident and told me to call him when I felt up to it.

I returned his call, and we booked a meeting for the following morning. I mentioned in passing that I wasn't going to take any pills prior to the meeting, which Remy apparently didn't agree with. We fought over it until we reached a compromise that I'd take half of the normal dosage, and he'd come with me. I normally wouldn't have wanted a babysitter, but Remy never made it feel like that.

On the morning of the appointment, my head felt thick, though I wasn't nearly as disoriented as I'd have been with a full dose. The lower dose also meant more pain, though it was bearable enough. Remy and I took the train and arrived ten minutes ahead of schedule. He stayed back in the lobby while I went out back, greeting a few colleagues on my way to my supervisor's office. Roger Braddock's door was already open, but I still knocked.

"Come on in, Maxim. Close the door behind you."

I sat down in one of the wooden chairs in front of Braddock's desk. His office was small and looked disorganized, yet I knew from experience that the middle-aged man before me was anything but. I met his gaze and sat up straight out of respect, despite the fact that it made my shoulder scream.

"I'm terribly sorry about not calling sooner, sir."

He waved a hand in front of me, dismissing my apology. "No need. You could have died—I understand you taking some time to deal with that. How is your shoulder?"

I actively had to remind myself not to just shrug. "There was ligament damage. I'll have to do physical therapy to regain my range of motion and rebuild strength, but I should make a full recovery."

Braddock sighed and nodded, seemingly relieved. "That's good, son. I can't wait to have you back."

"I can come back early if you need me. I can't do much in the way of physical work, though I'm sure there's something—"

He held a hand up and shook his head. "I'm going to stop you right there. I'm guessing part of what you have to tell me today is that you're on work restrictions."

"Yes."

"Which is exactly why you're *not* coming back until you're medically cleared. Take the time you need to get better. You never take vacation time, and I know this isn't exactly a vacation, but try to relax. Your job will be here for you when you come back, Maxim." I nodded. Braddock clicked the end of his pen a few times before he tossed it on the spread-out papers. "Have you contacted workers' comp yet?"

"No," I answered, shifting uncomfortably.

"Why the hell not?"

"I thought it would be a good idea to speak to you first. I want to be as transparent as possible." That, and I didn't want Braddock to think ill of me. I wanted to return to my job when this was over.

"I appreciate that, but you didn't have to wait. You should give them a call today. I'd even recommend a workers' comp lawyer to ensure you reach a fair settlement with the insurance company. You did a brave thing and probably saved the kid's life. Don't feel guilty about calling them."

"How is William doing?" I hadn't seen him since the accident, though none of the messages from Braddock mentioned he'd been injured.

"He's good. He sprained his thumb when he hit the ground, but he's fine. He's here, actually—was lookin' to speak with you."

"I'd like that."

"I'll page him—tell him to go to the lobby. Don't need you wandering around the back with all the equipment and supplies." He smiled and he winked at me, and I knew our meeting was done.

I stood, cradling my injured arm. "I'll have my family doctor fax over all necessary documentation after I've booked an appointment." Braddock wasn't big on goodbyes—which served me just as well—so I turned to leave.

"One more thing, Maxim."

"Yes, sir?" I asked, looking back at him.

"I want you think about my offer some more. You can have a good future with this company if you want it." With that, he resumed his work, and I left.

William was pacing in the lobby when I returned. Remy was side-eying him and his knee was bouncing wildly, though he kept quiet. They both set eyes on me as I approached, and Remy's knee stilled. "Maxim—fuck, man, I'm so sorry," William said in a rush.

The blue splint on his hand immediately caught my attention, and I felt guilty for having hurt him. "I'm all right. I apologize about your thumb. I didn't mean to hurt you."

Remy snorted a laugh, and William stared at me blankly.

"Fuck my thumb—I'd probably be dead if you hadn't intervened. Thank you. Thank you so much. I won't be so careless again."

I smiled at him, then nodded and patted him on the shoulder before going to see Remy. I heard William head out back while I studied Remy's amused expression. "What's so funny?"

"You, Max. You got fucking impaled by a steel pole saving that guy, and you just apologized for accidentally hurting his thumb. You're adorable." Remy climbed to his feet with that grin firmly in place. He patted my chest then headed for the door. "Come on, big guy. Where to next?"

AT BRADDOCK'S SUGGESTION, we went to see a lawyer for a consult. She seemed to have a thorough understanding of workers' compensation cases and spoke of settlements, maximum medical improvement, and temporary total disability—it was a lot. Remy did nearly all of the talking for me, and I ended up retaining her services. The next step was to book an appointment with my doctor and call workers' compensation, but first I wanted to take Remy out for lunch as thanks.

Remy spent most of the drive looking out the window, occasionally glancing at me to ask about new shops and restaurants. When we drove through Chinatown, headed toward the South Side, Remy's looks my way lingered and a small crease formed on his forehead. Our cab pulled up in front of Ricobene's on West Twenty-Sixth, and I wondered if bringing him to our old date spot had been a horrible idea.

My foster parents lived in this area, so Remy and I used to frequent the place every week, whether it was just for a quick slice. Sometimes pizza at nine in the morning was the answer—especially when you were sixteen and didn't want to go home. We'd continued going there at least once a week up until Remy...

"Holy fucking hell. This place is still open?"

I nodded to Remy, paid the driver, then we got out of the car and headed inside the brick storefront. It was before eleven, and there were plenty of spots to sit thankfully.

"Jesus. Nothing has changed about this place."

Remy was right. Framed photos and articles adorned the walls and the main space was taken up by small square tables and dark, wooden chairs. We stepped up to order and both got the breaded steak sandwich and fries. Once it was served up, I led us to a table against the wall and nearly gasped when our knees bumped under the table. The smell of the food, his knees bumping mine under the too-small table, his smile...

"Fuck me—this is so good," Remy said, his words muffled from a rather large bite of his sandwich. "Do you still come here often?"

"Only if I'm in the area. I've had a few jobs in the area over the years—nothing like before."

"Before I left, you mean."

"Uh, yeah." My skin prickled, and my eyes darted around the room. No one was watching us, though.

"Don't worry. We're not gonna get into that here. Eat up before it gets cold."

I gave him a crooked grin then devoured my lunch like I hadn't eaten in a week. Remy asked me about my meeting with Braddock, and I recapped it for him, hesitating toward the end. He cocked his head at me, and I knew he was about to call me out for acting weird, so I just said it. "Braddock has been trying to get me to apply for a managerial role with the company. He thinks it would be good for me. It's a significant pay raise and a fantastic opportunity."

Remy snorted a laugh. "Yeah, sounds like it. Let me guess —you don't want it." I didn't have to answer; he knew damn well I didn't. "You didn't ask, but here's my take anyway. I think you should do it. I know why you don't want to, but I think you should. You're great at what you do—your boss wouldn't have suggested this if you weren't—and it almost seems like it would be…"

"Easier. Please, don't try to spare me. Say what you mean."

"Yes, easier, physically speaking. Psychologically, it'd be a lot fucking harder. Your aversion to being the center of attention would be tested daily, and I know that would be difficult for you. It has to be something you truly want or you'll be miserable."

I hung my head and groaned. That was exactly my problem. Any time attention had been on me in the past, it hadn't ended well. As I got older I tried my best to keep out of focus. It wasn't hard when I was next to Remy. If he were the sun, then I was one of the planets caught in his orbit. As much as I tried to hide, he strived to stand out—and he did. Always.

"Hey, don't get all sad on me. I'm not finished yet. It's going to be hard for you, but I know you can do it, and I know you can excel at it. You're not that same defenseless kid anymore, yet you still feel like him. I can promise you that no one looks at you and wants to laugh." He eyed me almost appraisingly, then quirked an eyebrow. "Definitely not."

"People know what this scar means," I said, referring to the scar on my lip. I didn't have to point it out.

"Gut reaction is that it looks sexy, Maxim. I hope you'll understand that one day."

I dropped the conversation after that. It was a disagreement we'd had before, and one I'd even had with Mac on several occasions. I'd always wanted to believe Remy when he told me I was sexy or whatever, but it wasn't how I felt. Getting stronger helped, though I clearly still had my hang-ups. Thankfully, we dropped the subject in favor of lighter topics for the rest of the meal.

Back at my apartment, Remy saw to it that I took more medication, then he bolted for the shower to warm up. I tried to convince him to get a coat while we were out, and he'd insisted my sweater was fine. He was usually a better liar than that.

While I had some privacy, I went into my closet and took down an old ring box I kept near the back of the top shelf. It was covered in dust but otherwise looked exactly as it had when I'd placed it there eight and a half years ago when I moved in. I flicked the box open with my thumb, revealing the two matching gold bands Remy and I had once worn. I'd started saving for those rings when I was fifteen and got my first part-time job. At that point I hadn't told Remy how I felt. I knew that one day I'd marry him—and we came so close.

I heard the shower turn off and scrambled to put the box back in the closet. Remy came in just as I closed the closet door. A white towel sat low on his hips, and his hair had been pushed back on one side as if he'd absently run a hand through it. Beads of water still clung to his gorgeous body and dripped from the ends of his hair.

"I forgot to bring a change of clothes in with me."

A small smile tugged at the corner of my mouth. "You always did."

"Some things don't change."

"Some do." I moved away from the closet and headed for the door, though Remy didn't move aside. He took hold of my hand and laced our fingers together before drawing our joined hands up to his mouth. He kissed the back of my hand, then looked up at me with the saddest eyes.

"I'm sorry, Max. I—"

"I already know you're sorry. Just tell me why. Please."

Remy pulled his hand from mine and looked away. His jaw twitched while he ground his teeth. I didn't think he'd answer me, then he rolled his shoulders and looked me in the eye. "I wasn't ready. I thought I was, and I wanted to be, but I wasn't."

"Why not just tell me that?"

"I panicked. I didn't know what to say, and I couldn't face you."

"Is that all of it?"

He maintained eye contact with me and nodded, and I knew he wasn't being entirely truthful. Something had to have happened that shook him to the core, and it was bad enough that he didn't want to tell me. Or didn't feel he could. Considering he'd just lied to my face, it was clear I wasn't going to hear the whole story by continuing to push. I'd give him more time, and hopefully he'd tell me on his own.

"Okay," I replied, moving to step around him. He put his arm across the doorway, blocking me.

"You were perfect." He eyed me appraisingly from head to toe, then back up again. "You still are, Max. Don't ever doubt that." He lowered his arm, then waited, all the while keeping his heavy-lidded eyes on me.

He was flirting with me, and I knew it was a distraction,

but I didn't care. I grabbed his waist and pulled him against me, nearly crumbling to my knees when he gasped. His chest heaved against mine, and his hands trembled on my waist. Thinking I misread the situation, I went to step back, but his grip tightened, then his lips were on mine. He tasted like mint and my long-lost salvation. My fingers dug into his hip and I deepened the kiss, needing more of him.

It felt so good to touch him again—*really* touch him. I'd have sold my soul for the use of my dominant arm if it didn't already belong to Remy. He stood on his toes and pulled me down to him for more. His kiss was greedy and full of the same need I felt down to my core. I lost track of time—of everything—until my lungs burned for a breath.

We broke apart long enough to take a few breaths before Remy's mouth sought mine out again. One of his hands was under my shirt, scratching my back while the other tugged at the short hair above my nape. I backed him against the door-frame and tried to reach for his neck when a sharp pain in my shoulder made me cry out.

Remy pulled back, his brow furrowed in concern. "Fuck, did I hurt you?" I shook my head. My jaw was clenched tight to keep my teeth from clattering from the pain. "Get in bed. I'll be right back."

I did as I was told even though there was no way I could fall asleep. Between the pain and rush from kissing Remy, I was wide awake. Remy returned with a glass of water and an ice pack. Still clad only in a damp towel, he sat on the edge of the bed and gently pressed the ice pack against my shoulder.

"Trying to move was stupid," he said with a crooked grin.

I huffed out a short laugh and let my head fall back against the pillow. "I was a little preoccupied and not thinking straight."

"That so? And what were you trying to do?"

My cheeks burned, but I didn't look away. "I wanted to grab your neck. You always loved that."

He hummed. "Would you have told me I was yours? I always liked that too."

"Are you mine?" I hated how unsure I sounded. Even more, I hated that I'd asked him that. I'd inadvertently put him on the spot in the midst of a very complicated situation. And I didn't want to hear the answer.

Remy raked his teeth over his bottom lip, then cocked his head to the side. "I've always been, and will always be, yours. No matter where we are or how much time's passed."

The confusion whirling inside me multiplied by tenfold, yet I oddly felt a sense of comfort. Despite the time and the distance, I still had him. We clearly had more to unpack, but I hadn't lost him. I turned my hand palm up on the bed, then smiled when Remy put his hand in mine.

"Don't look too happy, big guy." He nodded toward the dresser. "I'm putting you on a full dose until whatever you messed up is better. And don't you dare try to say you're fine." He waited for me to nod before he pulled his hand away and took out two tablets. "We'll talk about what happened after you've had some rest."

He set the pills in my hand, and I took them without a fight. My left hand was free, yet he held the glass of water for me while I drank. A faint crease appeared between his brows, and I could only guess at the number of things weighing on his mind after what had happened just now. I didn't fully understand it myself, but I was happy to do whatever he needed and not fret over the details until we had a chance to talk about it.

"Will you lie with me?"

Remy bit his lip again. "I don't know if that's wise."

"I won't try anything."

"It's not you I'm worried about," he muttered. I slid my

hand over his and rubbed the inside of his wrist with my thumb. "Fuck. Fine—but I'm putting pants on."

I looked away and slid over while Remy got dressed. He came back and crawled right into my embrace, settled against my chest. The sound of him breathing, his scent, and his weight against me all reminded me of how things had been, and how they still could be. Perhaps it wasn't possible to pick up where we left off, and maybe Remy didn't want to. I'd find out when I woke, so I tried to enjoy the moment as best I could. I fought against the drugs until my lids were too heavy to stay open, and I let Remy's breathing carry me away.

SEVEN

REMY

I'D LIED AGAIN. It alarmed me how easily I could when I convinced myself it was for the best. What I told Maxim was only half of the truth, and it wasn't the worst half. As much as I'd like to pretend that I didn't know what came over me when I was giving Maxim my best "fuck me" eyes, I couldn't. The thought of him walking away upset after we'd shared such a nice morning didn't sit well with me. His smile was the most beautiful sight for my eyes, just as much as seeing him sad felt like a dagger in my heart.

I wasn't trying to manipulate him with the allure of sex— not entirely. I knew he wanted me, and I wanted him more. I'd only been ignoring my feelings to keep things from getting messy. It was so very clearly a bad idea, but I was the king of making those. Maxim was a tactile, affectionate person once he trusted you; it was killing him not being able to have intimate contact with me. Not necessarily sexual, though that was what had been driving me. I thought if this one bad decision would make us both happier, even for a moment, it would be worth it.

Maxim never would have made a move without my

consent, and I needed him to come to me. I practically laid myself out for him, and I had no shame about it. When he grabbed me, I wanted to melt against him. When he kissed me, I thought I had. Kissing Maxim had felt so natural—like the wasted years hadn't changed a thing. I wanted everything from him, and I would have taken it had he not hurt his shoulder.

When I woke up nuzzled against Maxim's chest, I felt so disgusted with myself. What the fuck would I have done if we hadn't stopped? I couldn't mess this up. Thinking about the consequences of my actions was another weakness of mine. Being reckless was my standard operating practice; I shouldn't have been surprised by my actions and desires. I was there to take care of him, and I'd remind myself of that every day if I had to.

I got out of bed to get a start on supper and put some distance between Maxim and me. Putting pants on hadn't stopped me from waking up all boned-up, so I left to go calm the fuck down. My culinary skills had improved slightly, though I was still pretty shit and stuck to basic meals. I finished all the veggie prep and was frying diced steak when I caught sight of Maxim leaning in the doorframe in my periphery.

"Hey, feeling better?"

"Hazy," he slurred.

"What about your shoulder?"

"Doesn't hurt at all."

I rinsed my hands, then dried them on a dish towel before going over to him. His pupils were huge, making his already dark eyes appear black. I quickly realized he wasn't leaning to look sexy. After a little convincing, I led him over to the couch and sat him down before he fell over. It baffled me that such a big guy could be taken down by such small pills, but I wasn't a fucking doctor, so what did I know? My only personal experience with pills came from oxy and molly, so I was hardly in a position to understand why drugs hit Maxim so hard.

Supper turned out okay, though it would have been better if Maxim had made it. We finished eating and were watching *Supernatural* after calling and booking an appointment to see Maxim's family doctor. Well, I was watching it. Maxim was lying down half on top of me with his head on my stomach, and he was asleep. I was half lying down myself, slouched low in a position that would have my mother chastising me. Kincaids were to be presentable at all times, and that included having perfect posture. Slouching was the least of my disappointments to my parents—the most by far was the gorgeous guy asleep in my lap.

They didn't care that I was gay. On the contrary, they fully supported my "alternative lifestyle" and donated vast amounts of money to LGBTQ charities. Me being gay was fantastic for the family's public and social image—so long as my partners conformed to my mother's standards, which Maxim did not. She wanted me with someone similar to me in social status, with the Ivy League education I was meant to have. In other words, a basic, boring, rich guy.

She'd loved Maxim while he was my best friend, then that changed overnight when we became lovers. She tried to blame him for my rebellious behavior, but I'd been like that long before I met him. I was never going to be the media friendly son they wanted. Then when my sister turned fourteen, she decided she didn't want to be the perfect daughter and turned into a punk princess with a penchant for black eye shadow. I, of course, got blamed for that.

"That feels good."

Maxim's deep voice startled me, though not enough to make me jump. No, it made me want to purr. "What does?"

"Your fingers."

My brows drew together in confusion and I was about to ask what the hell he was talking about when he nuzzled against my hand—which was apparently resting against the back of his head, playing with his hair. My fingers stilled at the same time a surprised "Oh" fell from my lips.

"You don't have to stop. I don't want you to."

His tone and heavy-lidded eyes conveyed the obvious meaning behind his words. I swallowed hard and put on my best poker face. "You're high as fuck right now. Perhaps this isn't the best time to finish our... talk from earlier."

"I disagree."

"It's not a good idea. You'd agree with me if you had a clear head."

Maxim grinned and bit his lip sinfully slow. "You're a bad liar, Remy. I can hear your heart beating." His hand thumped lightly on his chest in time with my racing heart. "Try again, love."

I sucked in a sharp breath and closed my eyes. "We can't get back together, Max."

"Okay."

"I'm not... I just can't, and I need that to be clear." I felt his fingertips tracing my jawline, the touches so soft they tickled. My cock stirred and began to fill.

"I understand," he replied as his fingers traveled down my neck and chest, pinching my nipple over my shirt.

The moan that fell from my lips was full of need—something I hadn't recognized in my voice in ages. Maxim pinched me again, and my hard cock twitched while I moaned. Before I could stop myself I was lifting my hips, seeking any sort of friction in pants that were way too baggy for me.

"Let me take care of you." Maxim began to sit up, but I

pushed him back down. He cast confused, dark eyes up at me but didn't try to move again.

"We can't fuck. Not until your shoulder is a bit better."

"You mean we can't until I'm no longer taking my medication."

"Yeah, that's what I mean." There was no use denying it.

"I'm not going to change my mind, but we can wait if that's what you want."

I didn't miss the clear disappointment in his voice, nor did I miss the outline of his thick cock straining the fabric of his sweats. While it was true that we should wait, I wasn't a fucking saint. Seeing Maxim hard and wanting me was too much to say no to. Rejecting him after *I* had started teasing would be a dick move, and I'd hurt him enough already.

"Maybe you won't. Just stay there for now." I slid my hand down his chest and under the elastic waistband of his pants. Maxim's eyes closed and his breath caught as my fingers wrapped around his cock. The feel of him hot and hard in my hand was absolute perfection. I didn't have the patience to tease him, and his rapid breathing and pleading eyes told me he didn't either. With a firm grip, I slid my hand up Maxim's cock, pushing his foreskin over his sensitive tip, then reversed the motion with less pressure. I continued my measured strokes and held him down with my other hand while he writhed in my lap. Restraining his powerful body gave me a rush I'd long forgotten, and the longing in those near-black eyes staring up at me told me Maxim felt it too. Without taking my eyes off of his, I swiped my thumb over his cockhead, and nearly came in my pants when his expression went slack and his eyes widened.

I wanted to kiss him so fucking badly, but I was transfixed by his gaze. Maxim looked at me like he used to—like I was his entire world. It flooded me with warmth yet also with longing for all that I'd deprived us of. I saw moments passed, and ones stolen from a life that could have been ours. And then I felt his fingers brush my cheek, and I saw only him.

"Remy," he moaned.

I worked my hand faster, bringing him to the edge in a matter of seconds. His body tensed and he bit down on his knuckle as he spilled into my hand. I stroked him through his orgasm, milking every last bit of pleasure out of his release until he became oversensitive to my touch.

My own cock ached, though I ignored it. I'd take care of it once Maxim drifted off. I withdrew my hand from his pants then licked my fingers clean while he watched me. "You taste just like I remember."

His eyes darkened and his gorgeous chest heaved. I thought he might say something when his lips parted, but his tongue darted out to lick them, and he remained silent aside from his heavy breathing. I took hold of his hand and kissed the back of it before resting our joined hands on his chest.

"Let me up. I'll get the shower going."

Maxim sat up, and I tried to do the same, but he pushed me back against the cushions. I narrowed my eyes at him in question as he shifted off of the couch and knelt between my spread legs, then his intent became way too clear. I wanted to tell him he didn't have to—I wanted to tell him to suck my fucking cock. My throat constricted, and I couldn't say either. Maxim didn't wait for words that wouldn't come. He pulled my pants down enough to free my cock, then his mouth was on me. He took me all the way down in one go, and I almost fucking blew.

I hissed at the exquisite heat and pressure and resisted the urge to grab his head and fuck his throat mercilessly. He'd give me what I wanted in his own time. I lifted my shirt with one hand and buried the other in his thick, short hair. His eyes flicked up and locked with mine while he tongued the underside of my cock, and a grin tugged at the corner of his mouth. I squirmed and groaned when he pulled back, keeping me from thrusting into his mouth.

"Max, come on." My voice was whiny and desperate even to my own ears. Maxim's grin widened. Frustrated and horny weren't states for me, so I stopped moving and started begging. "Please."

"Please what?"

"Suck my fucking cock."

He hummed before taking me into his mouth again—all the way down until his trimmed beard tickled by balls. I was close to coming from merely having watched him get off and wasn't going to last. Maxim must have known, because he didn't stop working me over, even when he gagged a couple of times. I didn't warn him before I came. It happened so fast; I couldn't do anything but close my eyes and cling to him as if he could keep me from being swept away in the whirlwind.

My cock pulsed in his mouth while his hand massaged my thigh, easing the tension out of it. When I opened my eyes, Maxim was looking up at me expectantly, and I noticed some of my cum dripping from the corner of his mouth. I leaned forward and swiped it away with the pad of my thumb, then smeared it across his lips. I traced the scar on Maxim's upper lip leading up to the bottom of his nose. His back stiffened and his eyes turned fearful, though he didn't pull away from me. I brushed his scar again, and his lips trembled.

"You're so gorgeous, Max." I swept my thumb over his scar again then his lips parted on a shudder. "Every inch of you is beautiful." He closed his eyes and remained still, despite how much I knew he wanted I pull away. I seized that opportunity to lean in and steal a kiss, drawing a surprised gasp from him. The taste of my cum on his lips surprised me initially—it wasn't as bitter as it usually was, which I could likely attribute to my healthier diet since cooking for Maxim. The longer we kissed the more that bitterness faded and gave way to a taste that was distinctly Maxim. *My* Maxim.

I pulled him up by the collar until he straddled me, and we continued to make out like we were lust-struck teens again. Maxim tried to keep his weight off of me, and I let him because I was too caught up in the moment. I'd always enjoyed the feel of his weight against me—a weight I longed to feel pinning me while his cock slid inside me and claimed me. He was big and powerful in ways I wasn't, yet he always treated me with care. Even when he was rough, he never did anything I didn't beg for.

Before I let him consume me completely, I broke our kiss and rested my forehead against his. A muttered "fucking hell" slipped past my lips, because what else could I say? Maxim nuzzled his nose against mine, then kissed me chastely before he rose to his feet. His jaw was clenched tight, though his eyes on me were kind and loving. I reasoned the tension in him was because his shoulder hurt, and not due to regret over what we'd done. At least not yet.

I tucked myself back into my pants—Maxim's pants— then led him to the bedroom. I tried to get in first, but Maxim's firm grip on my arm stopped me. "Wha—"

His soft kiss swallowed the rest of my words, and I let them go willingly. It was dark in Maxim's room, with only the dim lights from the city coming through the window. It was enough for me to make out his outline, though I was sure he smiled at me before he climbed into bed. He raised his left arm, wordlessly beckoning me to him, and I complied. With my head resting on his chest, I fell asleep almost believing we were twenty again, and that I hadn't fucked up the best thing that'd ever happened to me. Almost.

When morning came, I was scared to move. Maxim's

breathing let me know he was still asleep, and I was still cuddled against him. His arm was probably blue from lack of circulation, but checking would require moving, and that wasn't happening. If he was going to wake up and tell me to leave or look at me with shame in his eyes, I'd be crushed. Remaining glued to his side, breathing in his scent, was the safest option.

It wasn't long before Maxim roused from sleep and dispelled all of my worries with a simple kiss and a devastatingly handsome crooked grin. Light caressing to my rose tattoos let me know he still had use of his arm, and I bit back a grin. The urge to kiss him again and start some heavier shit swirled within me, but we had places to be. Maxim had an appointment to get his sutures removed, and we needed to get up. My half-hard morning wood could wait until we got back.

EIGHT

MAXIM

M Y FIRST FOLLOW-UP appointment with my doctor had gone well. My shoulder was healing nicely, and with the sutures gone, I no longer had to keep it wrapped. I'd still need a sling or brace for sleeping, but I could start doing simple tasks on my own again, like cooking.

Even so, Remy had insisted on making me sit and wait on the couch while he made supper. He'd been smiling more than he had since he'd arrived, but they were superficial at best. The lines around his eyes and the tension in his shoulders showed his true concern, and I knew why.

The other night had been a lot for both of us. Remy was probably right that the drugs had emboldened me, but I didn't care. I wanted him as much as I ever did, and no amount of medication could have changed my mind about it. Having Remy touch me like that again gave me such a heady feeling that I thought I'd pass out. His hand on my cock and his heavy grip on my chest had nearly unraveled me. After I came, I'd wanted him. Not just for the night— forever. If I were completely honest, I'd never stopped wanting him.

I knew he'd have put distance between us had I voiced my true wants, and I couldn't let him pull away. It seemed that Remy wasn't the only liar in this—whatever *this* was between us.

My doctor also said I could cut back on my pain medication, which was the best news. Second best was that I was cleared for light cardio and weights for my left arm, though he warned me not to overexert myself. Injuring my shoulder again would prolong my recovery, and possibly cause permanent damage. So I'd be patient and focus on what I could do instead of my temporary limitation. I'd texted Mac the good news after the appointment and he'd called back and announced we were going to the gym tomorrow morning. I was itching to get back and didn't put up an argument.

Remy had been distant, yet cordial, which only put me on edge. He was acting like everything was okay, when something was clearly bothering him. Waking up alone in bed all but confirmed my suspicions. Remy was many things, but an early riser was not one of them—when given a choice. This meant he'd been troubled and restless, or he was avoiding me. Or both. It was likely both.

The truth was I was nervous about seeing him too. Things would be different today, what with my doctor having effectively cleared me of needing Remy's help showering. A small flame of hope flickered deep in my gut that maybe he'd still want to shower with me now that it wasn't a necessity. He never used to like people knowing, but Remy was always a very introspective person. Clinging to the notion that he'd simply gotten up early to sort out his thoughts left me feeling more optimistic and ready to stop cowering away in the safety of my bed.

With one last mental pep talk, I carefully rolled out of bed, not bothering to remove the sling I'd slept in. After a quick stop in the bathroom, I found Remy sitting on the couch, clutching a coffee mug in both hands. His short hair was a mess, as if he'd been running his hands through it. I could picture him doing it, tugging too hard at the back as if the sharp pain would give him clarity. He hadn't seemed to notice me until I was standing next to him and wishing him a good morning.

His blue eyes turned to me, wild and unfocused for a beat before they softened with recognition. "Oh, hey. I didn't hear you come out. I didn't wake you, did I?"

"You know you didn't. Do you mind if I sit?"

"Shit, sorry," he said as he scooted toward the middle of the couch.

I slid in next to him and was about to ask him if he'd eaten yet, when I noticed that there wasn't any steam coming from his coffee. I took the mug from his hands, which were also cold. "Jesus, Rem, how long have you been sitting out here?" I rubbed my hands over his, ignoring how the action bit at my shoulder.

"I must have lost track of time." He shrugged, trying for nonchalance. "Had a lot on my mind this morning."

"Is this because of the other night?" *Of course it is.*

"Kinda. Not really. I don't really know."

"We don't have to talk about it right now if you don't want to, but I really think you should get warmed up..." I paused, my confidence fleeting. "Do you want to take a shower with me?"

He cocked an eyebrow at that. "You don't need my help with that anymore. Doc gave you the all clear, remember?" He was smiling, but it didn't come close to reaching his eyes.

I nodded, not quite ready to speak. I turned his hands in mine until they were palm up, and then stroked my thumbs over the undersides of his wrists. "I-I know that. I don't want you to help me. I want you *with* me—like we used to be."

"Max—"

"No." I gave his wrists a quick squeeze so he met my eyes and would know that I was serious. "If you don't want this, then tell me outright. Don't make up excuses. I heard your terms loud and clear last night, and I still accept them. It's okay if you've changed your mind, but don't say no because you somehow think it's what's best for me."

I'd said it. Without the cover of darkness or drugs to give me a boost in confidence, I'd told him I wanted him. Not to the full extent, but it would have to be enough until he was ready for more.

"Fucking hell. All right. You win." The corners of his eyes crinkled before they settled on my mouth.

I didn't wait for him to change his mind. With more force than necessary, I pushed forward and crashed my lips to his in a kiss we'd both be feeling later. He tasted like bad coffee, yet it was somehow perfect and everything I needed. He moaned when my tongue grazed the roof of his mouth, and I echoed the reaction when he did the same to me.

A low growl rumbled in my throat when Remy suddenly pushed me away, though he was forgiven a moment later when he settled in my lap. He fisted his hand in my hair and yanked my head back hard, then used his leverage to deepen our kiss. The sting of pain sent a jolt right to my cock, which was now half-hard. With only thin pajamas between us, Remy had to have noticed, and I knew he had a moment later when he ground his ass into my lap and smiled against my mouth.

He nipped all over my neck and earlobes, already so familiar with all of the places that made me squirm most. I'd closed my eyes while he reacquainted himself with my sensitive spots, reveling in his smell and how good his touches and bites felt.

He pulled back long enough for me to open my eyes and see the overwhelming need in his eyes peering into mine. His heavy gaze dropped from my eyes to my lips and back again so fast that I could almost convince myself that it had been involuntary. But I knew it wasn't. Before I could stop him, he leaned into me and nipped and licked the scar on my upper lip.

I wanted to come. I wanted to hide. More than anything, I wanted him. I shifted Remy to my left side, secured my good arm under his ass, and stood us up. He instinctively wrapped his legs around my waist, though his expression sobered.

"Your shoulder!"

"I don't need two arms to carry you, love."

He buried his head in the crook of my neck and muttered, "Jesus fucking Christ," while his hands found purchase around my neck and in my hair. "I'm going to kill you if you hurt yourself trying to be sexy."

"Trying?" I asked as I carried him down the hall. "I thought I was doing better than that."

He groaned. "Now you're making cocky jokes? You've been spending too much time with Mac."

"Please don't mention Macalister at a time like this." I eased my hold on Remy and let him slide down to his feet. "I want to focus on only you."

"Okay, big guy," he said before his lips gently pressed against mine. His fingers skilfully unfastened my shoulder sling, and let it drop to the floor. Instead of kissing me again or further undressing me, he studied my arm and shoulder, mapping out the dips and curves of the muscle. Fingers and lips traveled over my skin, the touches so light they almost tickled.

The sloppy, frenzied groping from the living room felt like a distant memory while Remy lavished me in feather-light caresses that oversensitized my skin. When he had me on the edge of begging, he stepped back and turned the water on. I couldn't drag my eyes away from him as he took off his clothes and stepped under the stream. As I stood transfixed by the beads of water flowing over every inch of his body, I was never more grateful to have transparent glass shower doors. The water made his tattoos look that much more stunning, and I wanted to trace each of them with my fingers—especially the roses on his back.

"You comin' in?" Remy flashed me a wolfish grin that had me shedding my pants like they were on fire.

In four long strides I was pressed up against him under the almost-too-hot water. He turned toward me and slipped his arms around my neck, pulling me down for a lazy kiss. I let him lead as I wrapped my arms around my waist, pulling him closer. The glide of his slick body against mine had me on the verge of coming within minutes. When I tried to pull back and warn him, his grip on me tightened, holding me in place.

Remy ground against my cock harder, but at the same slow, torturous speed until I shuddered and stilled as my orgasm nearly knocked me to my knees. Neither of us had remembered to turn on the fan, and the bathroom was small and didn't take long to fill with steam. Between the steam and coming so hard, I was dizzy on my feet. Remy steadied me while he smeared my release over my stomach, then his own cock.

"You're so fucking sexy, Max," he panted, stroking himself faster and faster.

I wanted to taste him again, but my head was still spinning. Remy's breathing picked up and he rested his forehead on my chest while his free hand was braced against the wall by my head. With nothing more than a strangled grunt, Remy's release mixed with mine and slid down my stomach.

Once he caught his breath, he scratched his fingers across my nape and chuckled.

"What's so funny?" I asked.

He shook his head, brushing it against my chest, before pushing off the wall and looking up at me. "I was just thinking about those awesome cum-gutters you've got." He trailed a finger over my abs then brought it up to his mouth and sucked. "We taste pretty fucking good. I'd offer you a taste, but I'm feeling kinda greedy right now."

I didn't even try to respond. My cheeks burned, and it had nothing to do with the steam.

"Yeah, I know you like it. You don't have to say anything." Remy pushed up onto his toes and kissed me. He took his time and made sure I got to sample the taste of us that lingered on his tongue. When he lowered back down to the tiles and moved away, I whimpered at the loss of him.

"Relax. I'm not going anywhere. I got you all dirty—the least I can do is clean you up." He winked at me while he rubbed the soap between his hands, working up a fragrant lather.

The first touch was to my neck. He massaged the soap in so gently that I could have fallen asleep if not for the effort it took to remain on my feet. Warm, slippery hands smoothed down my shoulders, lighter on the right side. We'd done this many times before, though Remy had used a cloth before and had stuck to the places I couldn't reach. This time was different. The way his hands smoothed over every inch of me almost felt reverent.

I closed my eyes and let him have his way with me. Remy's hands swept across my chest and stomach, down each of my legs, and even the soles of my feet, where he deliberately tickled me. I was still smiling from the tickle when he grasped my spent cock in one hand and twirled his fingers through my pubic hair with the other. A sigh rumbled in my throat, followed by a longer one when the hand in my pubes moved down to take hold of my balls. His slippery grip as he massaged them felt utterly divine. I wouldn't get hard again so soon, but damn if it didn't feel good regardless.

I was so distracted that I didn't notice his other hand had slipped back into my crease. A sharp gasp escaped me when Remy brushed his finger against my hole.

"Nice to see you're still so sensitive." He pressed harder and I moaned, fisting his hair with both hands. "Turn around. I need to get the back."

Remy withdrew his hands, and I did as he'd instructed. He rose behind me and I heard him lathering up again before his hands gave my back and ass the same thorough attention he'd given my front. He'd even washed my hair, though I had to bend down when his arms got tired from reaching. When he finished with me, he booted me from the shower and quickly washed up. Watching him gave me a semi that I was able to—kind of—hide with the towel tied around my waist.

I leaned against the sink and took him in from head to toe. For how gently he'd treated me, he was rough and fast with himself, which was more his style in general. Remy turned toward me and stepped out of the running shower while he smoothed his bleached hair back with both hands. I held a towel out for him, which he took and tossed over his shoulder. He shooed me away from the door and breezed out into the hall with a billow of steam following him. I looked toward the open door, then back at the running water before opting to shut the water off.

I listened for Remy but didn't hear anything, so I went after him. "You're dripping wet. What are you doing?" I followed the wet footprints to my room and found Remy sitting on his towel at the edge of the bed, legs spread wide, and his hand leisurely stroking his cock to full hardness.

My mouth went dry, and I froze in the threshold.

"Come 'ere. I've been waiting too long to get that monster cock in my mouth again."

Well. That got me moving.

"Dude, are you sure you're good to be here?"

I turned to Mac, careful to keep my left hand on the handle of the stair climber I was using and narrowed my eyes at him.

"Fine, fine. I'm just asking. It's only been a few weeks."

In truth, I loved that Macalister cared about me the way he did. He could be overbearing and intrusive at times—most times—but his heart was in the right place, and I could never be angry about that. "I saw my doctor a couple of days ago. I'm cleared for light cardio and weights on my left arm."

He sighed. I couldn't tell if it was in relief or over having to do more cardio than he'd like. "Well, you could have just led with that, you cryptic bastard."

The timers on our machines went off, and we slowed for a quick cooldown before hopping off. After one-armed rowing and the stair climber, I was exhausted. Three weeks without a proper workout was too long.

Macalister tapped me on the chest with the back of his hand, a casual gesture that normally would have landed on my arm. Had it not been in a brace. "Wanna hit the bike today too? Or have you had your ass kicked enough today?"

The corner of my lips turned up in a grin, and I shook my head.

"Yeah, I thought so. Shower time?"

"Actually, do you mind helping me stretch? Remy usually does it, but we didn't have time this morning."

Macalister raised his eyebrows at that. "Oh? And where is dear Remington Steele today? I was half expecting to see him standing there, scowling at me when I picked you up."

"He said he'd do some cleaning and make lunch."

"Mm-hmm. I bet." I went to my back while Mac knelt between my legs. "We both know he bailed because of me. Come on, hands on your stomach." Once my hands were in place, Mac lifted one of my legs, bent it at the knee, and pushed it toward my chest. "Which I can't for the life of me understand, by the way. The guy has no good reason to hate me. Me, on the other hand…"

"I don't understand why you two can't get along."

His head lolled to the side without a trace of amusement. "Really, Maxim? You can't think of *one* reason why I might not want to see his stupid, rich-boy face?"

I snorted a laugh. "What does that even mean?"

Mac switched legs and strummed his fingers absently on my raised thigh while he spoke. "You know what I mean. He's got that pretty-boy-rich-guy face that you just want to punch. And he's a selfish dick, so there's that too."

"Remy isn't selfish. And he's not some entitled brat, either."

"Here we go. You're always defending him. Did he tell you why he left?" Mac asked as he released my leg and switched back to the other.

I couldn't answer that. My throat felt like it was closing in on itself, and I could barely breathe, let alone speak.

"Yeah, I didn't think so. Come sit up for a minute." Mac reached a hand out for me, which I took, letting myself be pulled up. He handed me a water bottle and waited for me to finish drinking before he spoke again. "I know he's important to you. I don't mean to be such a jerk and make you feel bad. But, Max, you have to understand where I'm coming from. It isn't a place of judgment or malice. I just care about you too much to see him break you again."

There was no use denying it. Remy had broken me, more than I'd ever admitted.

"Be careful with him," Macalister added gently. "Don't rush in blind and get swept up in having him around again."

Does he know? He can't know. My heart hammered in my chest, loud enough that I was sure Macalister could hear it over the music and idle chatter in the gym. *He couldn't know. I haven't said anyth*—"Relax. Don't bother trying to deny it. You have Remy-sized bite marks on your thighs."

My eyes went wide, and I didn't even try to resist looking. There they were, just above the hem of my shorts. Two bite marks on my left inner thigh, and one on the right that was already bruising. My face flamed, and my attention darted around the room to all of the people in our vicinity.

A warm hand closed around the back of my neck, and my focus narrowed enough to see Mac smiling sympathetically at me. "It's all right. No one can see them. I only saw when I was stretching your hamstrings. Your shorts more than cover them, so unless you're planning on spreading for everyone in here, no one else is going to know." He grinned at me, easing my rising panic and making me snort.

I shoved him back and shook my head, trying not to smile while he laughed. Once he regained a semblance of calm, he motioned for me to get on my back again. Halfway down, I rested on my left elbow, and looked him in the eye. "Thank you—for distracting me."

"Anytime, Maxy."

I cringed, falling to my back with a thud. "You promised not to call me that."

"Did I? Must have slipped my mind. How about this," Mac started as he pushed a leg back and held it. "Tell me what you horny teenagers have been up to, and I'll stop calling you Maxy." The smug smirk on his face had me wanting to strangle him, but that didn't change the fact that the bastard got me.

I huffed and turned away from him.

"Yeah, that's what I thought, *Maxy*."

MACALISTER DROPPED me off at home a few hours later. He'd insisted on carrying my bags up for me, despite my insistence that I could handle it. When Remy opened the door and Macalister stuck his tongue out at him, it was clear why he really wanted to carry my stuff. I squeezed past Remy, who was also making faces at my ridiculous friend, and took the turquoise box in my hand to the yummy-smelling kitchen. After some heated whisper-shouting, the door slammed and Remy stormed into the kitchen with my gym bag and the store bag from Macy's.

"I hate that prick," he muttered, dropping the bags by the entryway before joining me by the counter.

I bit back a smile and pushed the box toward him. "I have something for you." He eyed the box suspiciously then flicked his gaze back to me. "It's not going to bite."

More mutterings about Macalister flew out of his mouth as he turned the box toward himself and lifted the lid. Inside the box was an assortment of gourmet donuts and cupcakes from Bryan's bakery. The stunned silence and sharp inhale told me I'd chosen the right thing; Remy still had a weakness for sweets.

"Oh my fucking God. These look *amazing*. Where did you find these?"

"Bryan. I don't know if you had a chance to meet him at the hospital, but he owns a bakery. They taste even better than they look." I pointed at the one simply glazed donut out of the dozen. "Those are my favorite."

He snorted and patted me on the chest. "Of course you like that one best. Thank you. I shoulda led with that, but thanks."

"I-I have something else for you as well." I stepped around him and grabbed the large white Macy's bag. I caught the reluctance in Remy's eyes and the slight shake of his head. "Please just accept these, and don't argue," I said as I handed him the bag.

He took the bag and crouched down to open it, first pulling out a black winter jacket and gloves. "You're too considerate for your own good, Maxim. You didn't have to buy me a jacket."

"It's cold out, and it's only going to get worse. You're not in California anymore, and you need a coat. And you said you wouldn't argue."

"I did not say that, but thank you." He peeked inside the bag, and a smile spread across his face. He scratched at his stubble and lifted the lid on the shoe box. "You got me some fucking Docs. Dammit—thank you."

He stood and flung his arms around my neck while mine went to his waist. "Thank *you* for taking such great care of me. I'm just returning the favor." I pressed my lips to his temple and hummed at the smell of my shampoo in his silky hair. "If either the coat or the boots aren't your style, we can exchange them."

"Nonsense. They're perfect. I used to have a pair of Docs just like those before—" His mouth snapped shut, and he shook his head. "Never mind." He dropped his arms and stepped back. "Ah, so are you hungry? I made roast chicken and veggies. It's not fancy, but I found a recipe for gravy, and that turned out pretty good."

Not wanting to start a fight, I let Remy's deflection slide and rubbed my stomach. "I'm starving. I only had a protein shake earlier."

"Go sit down, and I'll grab you some food."

Oh, right! "That reminds me. Thanksgiving is on Thursday. If you didn't have any plans with your family, Macalister

invited us to join his family for dinner. If you want."
Suddenly the laminate flooring was the most visually
engaging feature in my apartment.

"Mac invited us, or he invited you?" he asked with his
voice dripping with skepticism.

"He said you could come." *Begrudgingly.*

"If it's all right with you, I think I'll stay here. My presence would only cause drama."

I shook my head once before remembering that he
couldn't read my mind—even if it sometimes seemed like he
could. "Dubhlainn wouldn't let that happen. He has Macalister wrapped around his finger."

"Like a dog."

"Like a man in love," I corrected with the hint of a smile
tugging at my lips. "We don't have to go. I told him I'd ask."

"You can still go. I don't want you to miss seeing your
friends just to keep me company," Remy said, pulling two
plates from the cupboard.

I crossed my arms and waited for Remy to face me while
I searched for the right words. "Mac is like a brother to me,
Rem. He's been there for me over the years when I needed
him." Remy winced at that, but I wasn't finished. "Any
animosity he has toward you stems from how protective he is
of me. He's important to me, but so are you. I want to spend
Thanksgiving with you, whether we're here eating takeout or
at Mr. and Mrs. Buchanan's house, eating the most delicious
meal I've ever had."

"I could really go for some deep-dish pizza for the takeout. Especially after all this healthy shit you insist on," he
teased. He had both plates full and handed me the one with
nearly twice as much on it.

"Thank you. So, I guess you're not considering seeing
your family? What about Rosalind?"

He shook his head dismissively then headed for the living

room. "I'm not ready to see my folks. And Roz doesn't know I'm in the city."

I followed and sat beside him. "You should call her. She was pretty sad and angry when you left, but it was only because she missed you."

He sighed heavily, his shoulders slumping, and he dropped his fork on his plate before turning to me. "If I tell you I'll text Roz tomorrow, can we table further discussion about my family today? They're not what I want to think about right now." He slid a hand over my thigh, across the front of my pants, and squeezed. I swallowed hard and nodded. "Good boy."

Remy withdrew his hand and turned on the TV for more reruns before we dug into our late lunch. The easiness between us returned as we finished eating and snuggled close to watch more *Supernatural*. Not wanting to ruin the moment, I decided I'd tell him that Mac knew about us another day.

NINE

REMY

THE CAFÉ SMELLED STRONGLY of coffee and bacon and was nearly filled to capacity. I'd managed to snag a table for two in the back, and I sat with my back to the entrance. My nervous foot tapping was louder than usual, and I glanced down to see the new boots Maxim had picked up for me. I could have been at home with him, curled up in bed, sweaty and naked. Instead I was a jittery mess in desperate need of a smoke, waiting for my sister to meet me.

But that isn't really your home.

I scoffed under my breath. There was no way I could ever forget that little fact. Liars and cheaters like me didn't deserve to have that kind of home, no matter how much I wished things could be different. If I could be Marty McFly for a day and fix my wrongdoings, how different might my life be?

Life didn't work that way, though. Thinking about it was nothing more than self-flagellation without the kinky benefits. I washed the thoughts away with a swallow of my bitter black coffee, then pulled out my phone to occupy my restless hands.

My thumb hovered over the Instagram icon for a few beats before I swept past it and tapped on Reddit. I'd deactivated my Instagram account after my life imploded, but the habit of checking it was hard to shake. It was a reality that I needed to come to terms with, though. That wasn't my life anymore—really, it never was. It was something I did, but not who I was. In that regard, I was just as lost as I was at sixteen.

"Remy?" a familiar voice asked from behind me, startling me.

I turned around and was met with bright blue eyes the same shade as my own. "Hey, Roz." An awkward couple of seconds passed between us before I dropped my phone on the table and stood to give her a hug. Thankfully she returned it.

"I was shocked when you texted," she said, dropping her arms from my back and taking a seat across from me. "You back here for good?"

"No. I don't think so." *God, I could go for a smoke.*

"You kinda look like shit."

"That's what you have to say to me after four years?"

She shrugged. "You looked like shit four years ago in LA too. Note that you've upgraded to 'kinda look like shit' now."

I huffed a short laugh. "I'm not feeling the love here."

Roz cut her eyes at me, daring me to continue down that road.

"Okay, point taken," I replied quietly.

She sat back in her chair and hiked her left ankle up to rest on her right knee. With one arm hooked over the back of the chair, she looked completely carefree—exactly how I remembered her. She was just as short as she was the day I'd left Chicago when she was seventeen—all of five foot nothing. Small, but fierce.

"I didn't come here to make you feel like an asshole, but if you say stupid shit, I'm going to reply in turn."

"Okay, no more awkward bullshit."

She nodded at that with a pleased grin.

"I'm been a shitty brother, and I'm sorry for that."

"You're forgiven." Roz snorted softly at my wide eyes and fiddled at the large silver rings on her fingers with her thumb. "It's fine, Remy. We're both adults with our own lives, and I never blamed you for wanting to get out from Mom and Dad. It was pretty trash that you seldom answered my texts, but life goes on. We don't have to dwell on that. I'd much rather know what you're doing here now?"

"A couple of things. I got tired of—"

"Before you say whatever you're going to say, do know that I used to follow you on Instagram," she said with a lowered voice.

Fuck. "LA was a fuckin' disaster. I've been staying in Palm Springs with a friend." I rapped my knuckles on the table and chewed my bottom lip. "I'm back here because of Maxim."

Her thick, dark brows that belied her bleached hair color rose in surprise. "What's going on with Maxim? Anytime we've talked, you made it seem like you two weren't in contact any longer."

"He—"

Her phone rang, and she quickly tapped the screen to answer it. "Sorry, one sec," she mouthed. Her eye roll came seconds later, followed by her tapping "End Call" and setting her phone facedown on the table. "I'm really sorry about that. It's rude as shit, but I'm on call and have to answer."

"So, you're an actual doctor now?"

"I'm still a resident, but yes. I moved back here for the last year of my residency."

I puffed my cheeks and blew out a deep breath. "Crazy."

"Not as crazy as you being back here—get back to what you were saying about Maxim."

I should have known better than to try to distract Roz. She was always the smarter of the two of us, even from a young age. Her edgy look may resemble mine, but she wasn't a colossal fuckup.

"Max was in a work-related accident. He's okay," I added quickly, before she could panic. "His shoulder got hurt, so he's off until he's all healed up."

"Jesus fuck. When did this happen?"

I relayed the events of the accident, and how Maxim had been doing since then—leaving out the, uh, racy bits—until she was sufficiently up to speed. A server had come around with a coffee pot and filled the mugs on the table around when I was explaining Maxim's recovery timeline.

"Poor Maxy. Can you let him know I'd like to see him? We fell out of touch some years ago."

"I think he'd like that. It was actually his idea that I text you."

She lifted a brow and hummed. "Oh, really?"

"I was going to anyway... eventually." I raked a hand through my hair and groaned. "This shit is fucking hard, okay?"

"I know, brother. We're square as far as I'm concerned. I mean that."

A heavy, relieved sigh released the tension in my shoulders I hadn't realized I'd been carrying. "I don't deserve it, but I'll take it."

"Good boy." She sipped her coffee, and I did the same, missing the way Maxim's crappy blend tasted. "When did you two start fucking again?"

I choked. I fucking choked—full-on chest thumping and lack of oxygen. "What?" I asked, though it came out rough and gritty. I'd also burned my throat.

"You guys are soulmates. He's always loved you, for whatever twisted reason." She softened the words with a grin.

"Can we please talk about something else?"

"Fine," she agreed. Too easily. "Have you been to see Mom and Dad?"

Brat. "Do they want to see me?"

"Yes… Maybe. Fuck, probably not."

I grinned, matching her expression. "I'll go see Mom first. Don't tell them I'm back yet." I needed way more time before I'd be ready for that fucking nightmare.

"I take it you're not coming to Thanksgiving dinner tomorrow then?"

"No. I have plans with Maxim."

"All right. I won't mention you until you're ready."

Our server came back to take our orders, which Roz gave without a second thought. I hesitated, cursing my money woes. I hadn't told Maxim about the extent of how broke I was now, but he seemed to have an idea anyway. Before I left to meet Roz, he'd given me fifty bucks and told me to have a nice breakfast. Of course, I'd tried to refuse it, but Maxim was stubborn. I also didn't have any alternative.

"Um," I stalled. I eyed the cheapest option on the menu before it struck me that Maxim wouldn't be happy about it. He'd ask me about this visit when I got back, and if I said I'd ordered a side of toast, he'd be disappointed.

I closed the menu, handed it to the server, and ordered chocolate Belgian waffles with extra whipped cream and strawberries, and a double side of bacon.

ON THANKSGIVING we stuck to our plan and picked up pizza—pepperoni and double sausage—from Lou Malnati's on North Wells, along with a twelve-pack of beer. Maxim surprised me with another box of those glorious sweets from his friend's place, which he'd hid from me the night before.

"Does that bakery deliver? How did you get these?" I asked as I shoved a whole confetti macaron in my mouth. Heaven.

Maxim snatched the box from me and put it in the fridge, along with the beer and snacks we'd picked up. "I asked Macalister to swing by Eat Cake and get them. He likes to drive Dubhlainn to school when he can, and the bakery isn't far out of the way."

"To *school?* I figured he was young, but damn."

"College. He'll be twenty next month. You'd like him. You're both"—his forehead creased while he chose the right word—"spirited."

"Why do I get the impression you mean feisty and not enthusiastic?"

He smirked and shrugged, feigning innocence.

I grabbed the pizza boxes off of the counter and kicked him on the ass gently before moving into the living room. "I'll make you pay for that comment later," I called out as I sat down on the floor in front of the couch.

Maxim walked in a minute later balancing several cans of beer and my box of treats against his chest. He took a seat on the couch over my left shoulder and leaned forward to kiss my temple before handing me a beer. I had no doubt the sweet gesture colored my neck and cheeks; the tips of my ears felt aflame.

I wanted to crawl into his lap and have his hands all over me, and I would. As soon as we finished eating. Over ten years without a proper deep-dish pizza was too fucking long. The first bite of that thick, saucy, meaty monstrosity gave me extra motivation to show Maxim just how thankful I was later.

NOVEMBER ROLLED INTO DECEMBER, and another trip to the doctor confirmed that Maxim no longer had to be confined to a brace at all times. It would still be another two months before he could start with light workouts on it and he'd still have to wear it occasionally but this was great news.

We were sent home with a list of recommended stretches to maintain strength, flexibility, and range of motion, as well as a referral for a physical therapist. Max insisted on home care as much as possible, so seeing a professional every couple of weeks was necessary for his worker's comp. It also reassured me that I wasn't going to fuck up his recovery. The blind faith Maxim had in me only went so far to ease my doubts.

Maxim's doctor stepped out of his office to grab a business card for the physical therapist, leaving me alone with a hot, half-dressed Russian stud. *Yeah, great job keeping it professional, Rem.*

"Can you check and see what movies are playing? I don't want to keep you cooped up in my small apartment all the time," Maxim said sheepishly.

My fidgety foot stilled, and I looked up at him on the exam table. "I'm not being 'cooped up.' I love spending time with you at h—at your place." *Nice save.* I pulled out my phone and zeroed in on the screen, not wanting to know whether or not Maxim caught my near slip. "What genre are you in the mood for?"

He grunted noncommittally. It was my choice. I tapped the AMC app, but it wouldn't load. I tried Safari next and furrowed my brow when it too wouldn't fucking load. Then I noticed that I wasn't connected to a mobile network and it hit me.

Dread. My breath caught, and my fingers trembled. My

benefactor. My sugar daddy. My owner of sorts. *Stanley.* He must have canceled my phone service—the plan he'd taken out for me and had been paying for.

Fucking fuck! Why hadn't I considered this would happen? *Because you were too busy trying to live in your past.* What the fuck was I going to—

"What's wrong, love?"

I flinched, then shot my gaze to Maxim. He was studying me with slightly lifted, creased brows. He knew I was distressed, so I couldn't lie. But what could I say? The best lies always contained pieces of the truth. "Ah, sorry. My fucking phone isn't working. Mind if I use yours?"

Maxim eyed me up and down before he handed me his unlocked phone, which I took with strained thanks. "Please tell me what's wrong, Remy."

I squeezed the phone tight to keep my hands steady, and I forced my breathing to remain even by mentally counting backwards. *In—three, two, one. Out—three, two, one.* "I'm all right, Max. Hey, that new comedy with James Franco is playing. You used to have a thing for him when we were younger."

"You're still a bad liar," he replied.

The good doctor came back in, business card in hand, and saved me from lying to Maxim again. "Ah, sorry. I'm all finished with the examination. You can get dressed now."

Maxim nodded, then reached for his shirt with his now-freed right hand. It was a touch too far, and the extension made him wince.

I jumped up and grabbed the shirt, helping him into it. "Easy there, big guy."

"Yes, please do listen to Mr. Kincaid since you insist on not listening to me."

Maxim flushed. "Sorry, Dr. Wells."

"It's quite all right. See the nurse on your way out to schedule a follow-up in a month's time."

With a new appointment set and a movie picked out, we left the doc's office and spent the rest of the day deliberately not addressing the fact that I was the world's shittiest fucking liar.

TEN

MAXIM

For over a week I'd been trying to get Remy to come to the gym with me. Some days he spent time with his sister; otherwise he stayed at my apartment and watched TV or used his MacBook. I hated him being home alone, but I couldn't skip my workouts. Remy would have come along if I'd insisted or framed it as me needing his help, though that level of manipulation didn't sit well with me. I tried to respect his decision to not want to come, but that didn't stop me from asking in case he ever changed his mind.

"Are you sure you don't want to come today? Bryan will be there to entertain Mac if that's what your concern is." I leaned against the kitchen counter, watching him chop up a green bell pepper.

"It's not a good idea, Max."

"Okay. Oh, we need more groceries. Mac has a meeting to get to, and Bryan has to go back to work, so do you think you could meet me at the store?"

"For sure." His chopping faltered a moment then resumed. "Um, what time would that be?"

"I don't know exactly. I'll send you a text when we're finishing up so you can head over."

The knife came down hard, and I noticed his hands were trembling.

"What's wrong? And don't say nothing. You've been acting strange all week. Please talk to me, Rem." I was one step away from shamelessly begging him.

His Adam's apple bobbed, then he set down the knife. His gaze remained on the counter. "My phone isn't working. I wasn't able to pay the bill, and it's been shut off."

My brows knitted together, and I cocked my head slightly to the side. I had no doubt what he was telling me was the truth, though I didn't believe for a second that it was the *entire* truth. For whatever reason, Remy was withholding things from me. But what could I do? I had no right to demand he tell me. It was technically none of my business, no matter how much I wanted it to be. So I let his lies slide. What else could I do?

"Okay. Thank you for telling me." I tried to keep my tone light and even.

Remy turned his attention to me and narrowed his eyes ever so slightly. "That's it? You aren't going to ask why?"

"You've already told me you were having money troubles. I'm here to listen if you want to tell me more, but I don't want to push you, love."

He forced out a shaky breath and gripped the edge of the counter. "Thank you."

"Of course." I pushed off of the counter and swept in behind Remy, wrapping my arms around his waist, and pulling him against me. "I don't want you to take this the wrong way, but will you please let me get your phone reconnected?" He started to protest. My lips on his neck silenced him. "I need to be able to contact you. We're not always going to be together, and you need to have your freedom."

I rubbed the jut of his hip bones, and he sighed, melting against me. "All right, Max. Thank you."

"We can get it sorted out after the gym."

"I suppose I have to go now. Fucking hell," he muttered.

I hugged him to me and hummed, glad he caught on to what I was implying. It wasn't going to be as bad as he was assuming.

"I'M NOT gonna let a selfish dick like you win," Macalister panted, sweat dripping down his forehead.

"Go fuck yourself, Ken Doll." With his face reddened, and his arms coated in a sheen of sweat, Remy looked about ready to collapse. He and Mac exchanged a few more colorful unpleasantries as they scowled at each other from side-by-side stationary bikes.

Bryan's low chuckle grabbed my attention, and I turned back toward him. He was watching me, and not the other two like I'd been expecting.

"Your guy will be fine. You know that Mac is all talk, and even then, he's not very intimidating. Let them run themselves ragged, and they'll be too exhausted to bicker and go on."

I cleared my throat, embarrassed that Bryan had seen through me. "Remy isn't my guy."

"Sure he isn't. From what Mac's told me—which isn't much—I know it's complicated as hell. I'm not trying to pry, and I hope you don't think I'm overstepping, man. It's pretty damn obvious that there's something between the two of you." Bryan slowed his jog to match my walk then reached for his water bottle.

I grunted and nodded. There wasn't a point in denying what Bryan had said. It was all true. Remy and I had *some-*

thing going on, though I don't think either of us knew exactly what. We didn't talk about the physical aspect of our relationship anymore. It felt like so much more than merely fooling around, but not nearly enough.

I was sure Bryan could understand at least a bit after the waiting he did for Elijah when they were just friends. They had a fresh, innocent love that everyone else could see blossoming, even when they—Elijah in particular—couldn't. I didn't have that with Remy. What we had was messy and tainted from secrecy and a decade of distance. I couldn't wait and hope that everything would be okay.

Shouting from the direction of the stationary bikes caught my attention, and I craned my neck to see Macalister and Remy pushing and kicking each other while still trying to pedal.

Bryan groaned, then turned off his treadmill. "I should go break that up before they get kicked out or banned." He patted me on my left shoulder as he jogged off to go wrangle Macalister.

Bryan's chiding was too low for me to hear, though Macalister's protests followed by his defeated, "Yes, Dad" were crystal clear. I was smiling to myself when a warm hand settled on my lower back.

I spun around and found Remy, drinking from a water bottle. He looked… rough. With his chest heaving, his legs shaking, and sweat pouring off of him, he looked like he might actually pass out. Despite his state, he was still beautiful.

"I fucking hate the gym," he wheezed.

After turning off my treadmill, I stepped off, slung my left arm over his shoulders, then kissed his temple.

"Ew, don't kiss me right now. I'm all gross."

"You're always gross, fuckboy," Macalister said from a few feet away. He and Bryan were heading over to the weight machines—which I missed most. Bryan grabbed Macalister's ear and tugged, eliciting a yelp from our ridiculous, blond friend.

"What the hell was that for, dude?"

"I told you to stop acting like an asshat not even two minutes ago." Bryan dragged him away, then threw his arm around his neck and pulled Macalister close. He said something in a hushed voice I couldn't hear, and Macalister nodded.

"I like Bryan," Remy said. "I can see why you're friends with him. Still don't understand wh—"

"Rem," I warned.

"Fine. I won't say it. But we both know I'm thinking it, and that still counts." He stormed off and plunked down on a weight bench, dropping flat onto his back with his hands clasped behind his head.

I joined my friends a few benches away from Remy. Macalister was spotting for Bryan while he did bench presses. Sighing to myself, I picked up a forty-pound dumbbell, took a seat on a bench, and went to work on my good arm and shoulder.

DESPITE HAVING A WORKING PHONE AGAIN, Remy accompanied me to the gym twice more that week. He and Macalister had downgraded from manly competitions of endurance to childish stares and silly face-making. Whatever Bryan had said to him was clearly working. I'd have to thank him the next time I saw him—which would be soon considering how much Remy enjoyed his desserts.

An email from my financial advisor got me thinking more about my situation with Remy, and what I wanted for my future. She reached out quarterly and we sat down for a face-to-face to go over my investment portfolio. At thirty-two, I was far from retirement, but I had other goals. I'd started saving for a home as soon as I'd turned eighteen.

I was hoping to be able to surprise Remy on his twenty-fifth birthday with a place we could call our own. After he'd left, that plan fell to the wayside. I still saved most of the money I earned even if I hadn't seen the point in taking that next step. Apartment living wasn't something I wanted long-term, but it had been adequate. I didn't have much, and I hadn't needed it up until this point in my life.

It was far too soon to be thinking about the future with Remy, but I couldn't help it. No matter how much I told myself not to get too attached, it was pointless. I wanted him just as much as I ever had, and now I knew that that wasn't going to change.

I chose a day when Remy would be going to visit his sister at the hospital where she worked. Her schedule was a mess this week, so Remy said he'd go to her during one of her breaks. It hadn't snowed in the last week, so I walked to my bank. Of all the meetings I'd had with Meghan, this was the first one I was nervous about.

"You should come with me sometime to see Roz," Remy said from the kitchen as he washed our dishes. He passed me a plate to dry. "She asked about you again."

"I'd love to see Rosalind. I wanted to give you two a chance to reconnect."

He snorted. "If you call her Rosalind now, she might claw your eyes out. Then again, if anyone could get away with it, it'd be you." His brow furrowed then he shut off the water and turned toward me. "Why do you always use people's full names? You always have—except with me."

Because you're mine, was my first thought, though that

wasn't entirely it. He watched me intently while I searched for the right words, studying my face, then he grinned.

"Is it because I'm special?"

I nodded.

"Anything else?"

Another nod.

He cupped my jaw and brushed his thumb over my lips. He stopped at my scar and traced it, making me shiver. "What else is it, Maxim?" Remy brought his other hand up to my face and scratched at the thick scruff on my cheeks. "You haven't trimmed this since that night on the couch, huh?"

He didn't have to specify which night he meant. I always kept a few days' worth of growth, but since the night when Remy touched my scar, I'd been letting my beard grow to hide it. At least that's what I was hoping to achieve.

Remy tugged gently on my chin then let his hands drop. "Yeah, you fuckin' haven't. Come with me." He took my hand and led me out of the kitchen, past the living room, and down the hall to the bathroom. He flipped on the light and guided me to sit down on the closed lid of the toilet seat. "Stay put."

I watched in silence as he dug around in the cabinet behind the mirror, first taking out metal scissors, then shaving cream and a pack of disposable razors I'd forgotten I had. I always used an electric razor, which I kept under the sink.

"You look hot as fuck with a beard, but it's been a long time since I've seen you clean shaven." Remy picked up the scissors, and I froze. "What's that reaction for?"

I tried, and failed, to swallow the lump in my throat. I hadn't been clean shaven since I was eighteen; it drew far too much attention to my scar. I couldn't do that again. Having everyone stare at me would be too much to bear again. Panic began to lance through me. My pulse raced, and my skin felt too tight. I went to stand and was immediately pushed down by Remy's hand on my chest.

"It's all right, Max. I'm not going to hurt you." He let his fingers dance through my chest hair, down the middle of my pecs. He leaned in close and kissed me before dragging his lips to my ear. "I know you're scared. Do you still trust me?"

It was the second time he'd asked me that in the last few weeks, and my answer hadn't changed. "Yes."

"Then close your eyes and stay still for me."

I did as he asked and was lavished in kisses and caresses that went a long way toward easing my mind. I wasn't sure how much time had passed when he made the first trim. The falling hair tickled my chest and shoulders when it fell, but I kept my eyes closed as Remy had instructed. The clink of the scissors on the edge of the sink caught my attention before I heard Remy stand up and step away. He ran the water at the sink—hot, based on the steam making the air thick.

When he returned, he draped a warm, wrung-out towel around the lower half of my face and neck. Once it cooled, he removed it and rubbed my face and neck in a thick lather of shaving cream. The crinkle and rip of tearing plastic let me know he'd opened one of the razors. I waited for the first sweep of the blades, tense and still.

I jumped when Remy's weight settled in my lap. "Easy, big guy. Is this comfortable for you?" he asked, rubbing my sore shoulder over my sling.

I bowed my head once.

He dropped a quick kiss on the tip of my nose, then angled my head up to the side. The grainy scrape was loud in my ears as Remy made the first pass of the razor on my jaw. His weight shifted in my lap and I heard him rinse out the razor in the water-filled sink. He leaned back toward me and made another caring downstroke, and I felt myself wanting to melt against him.

With every pass of the razor, I sunk further and further from reality. I found myself underwater with Remy, holding him close, and kissing him like nothing else mattered. And nothing else did. He nipped my lower lip, and I whimpered, hungry for more—for everything.

"Where's your head right now?"

My eyes snapped open at Remy's question. His blue eyes stared into mine with amusement and something else I recognized. Lust.

"You must've been thinking about something good." He reached between us and squeezed my dick, which had hardened while my mind wandered. "Wanna share what's got you so hot?"

"You," I blurted out. "I use a nickname for you because it distinguishes you from everyone else. You're not just Remington to me. You're *my* Remy. My Rem. My love. No one else gets to have that but you." It was more than I'd meant to say. Once the words started, I couldn't stop them. This was his chance to run.

"Fucking hell, Max," was all he said before his lips collided with mine in a frantic, bruising kiss. His fingers worked through my hair and pulled my head back. Tears prickled the corners of my eyes from the sting, but my focus was solely on the man in my embrace. "You can't say shit like that to me."

"Take my sling off. Please." My voice dripped with desperation and need that had nothing to do with my shoulder.

Remy knew. He was so close now, just holding me still. His breath mingled with mine, and our foreheads touched, as if we couldn't get enough contact. "Max, we—"

"Take it off. Now."

His fingers fumbled while he unfastened the sling without looking. Before it had hit the floor, I had both arms tight around him and rose to my feet. Remy sucked in a breath and hooked his ankles behind me. With our faces so close together I couldn't help but kiss him, despite not being able to see where I was going.

I tripped on what had to be Remy's jeans from earlier and slammed him against the wall next to the bedroom door. Before I could think to pull back and ask if he was okay, he moaned low and deep and rolled his hips against my stomach. If Remy was in the mood for rough, I'd give it to him as best I could.

We made it to the bed without further incident. I threw him down and watched him squirm a moment before I was overwhelmed with one thought: his skin on mine. I stripped off his pants while he took care of his shirt. His hard cock still tall and straight, already glistening at the tip. I fought the urge to taste him long enough to shed my clothing and crawl between his legs. He'd showered this morning before he left, but his scent was still strong. My eyes rolled back as I nuzzled the junction where thigh met groin. I was instantly seventeen again—back on the first night I had Remy naked beneath me.

"Don't go daydreaming on me now," Remy said with his voice strained. He threaded his fingers through my hair and guided my mouth to his cock. "Make me scream, baby."

My lips closed around his tip and I sucked. Over the last week I'd rediscovered what Remy liked, and I pulled out all the tricks. Remy liked to be worked over slowly when it came to blowjobs, and I planned on giving him something to savor.

My tongue swiped over the sensitive underside of his cock just below the head while I kept up the light suction. Obscene sucking sounds mixed with Remy's moans filled the room and spurred me on. I took more of him in, slowly sinking down until he hit the back of my throat. The angle was off, and I was still too rusty for him to throat-fuck me, though I kept on pushing myself.

Remy's thighs trembled beneath me, and his breathing picked up. He was going to come soon, but I wasn't ready. I pulled off and was met with a frustrated cry and dagger eyes.

"What the fuck? Why'd you stop?" He started to sit up, and I pushed him back down.

"Don't move," I said as I rolled over to grab the lube from my nightstand. I came back and knelt between Remy's legs, rubbing one of his knees while I took in the gorgeous sight before me.

A grin turned up the corners of his mouth when he saw the lube in my hand. He fisted his cock at the base, then slid his hand up and down his length.

Not wanting to be distracted, I managed to tear my gaze away, then rubbed two pumps of lube over my index and middle fingers. Remy moaned louder, this time purposefully teasing me. His grin had grown wider and was now a self-satisfied smile, complete with a bite to his lower lip.

He was trying to rile me up, but it wasn't necessary tonight. I didn't think I could have taken him slow and gently if my life depended on it.

His smile morphed into a gasp when I pressed two fingers into him without warning, stealing the air from his lungs. I was fast and rough stretching him, but neither of us could wait. When he bore down and rode my fingers in time with my thrusts, I withdrew them.

"Maxim," he moaned, spreading his legs wider for me.

Remy was barely ready, but it had to be enough. I pumped out more lube and quickly slicked up my cock, then lined up at his entrance.

"This is going to hurt. You can hurt for me, can't you, love?"

"Fuck, yes. Do it, Max."

The fire in Remy's eyes was on the verge of engulfing me. I knew the risks of being with him, of what he could do to me. My whole world could go up in flames on his whim. I closed my eyes, pushed inside, and willingly chose to burn.

Perfect was the only way to describe how good it felt to be inside Remy again. The tight heat surrounding me was almost too much. His blunt nails digging into my back helped ground me, pulling me back into the present. Remy was tense under me, the tendons in his neck taut and strained. I shifted back slightly, and he sucked in a sharp breath that nearly matched the one he'd released when I penetrated him.

"Fuuucking fuck."

I nuzzled into his neck, nipping and kissing his tender skin until I made my way to his lips. "You feel so good, Rem." I pushed further into him and kissed him when he cried out again. "So damn good. Get ready to scream for me, love."

I snapped my hips into Remy fast and hard, and he did scream. I worried that I'd misread his wants after so long, then he hooked his legs together and his heels dug into my lower back. He wanted this just as much as I did, so I didn't hold back. I set a relentless pace that had him moaning and clinging to me with all of the strength he had, and which had my muscles burning with exertion.

Remy responded to every powerful thrust so beautifully. His voice had gone ragged from moaning and calling my name, but he didn't stop. I kissed him one last time then pulled out, causing him to wince.

With little effort, I flipped him onto his stomach and dragged him to his knees. After slicking myself with another pump of lube, I was back inside him, buried until my balls rested against his ass. I stayed up on my knees and used the leverage to give my shoulder a break while I nailed his prostate. Remy's hands scrambled for something to brace against, though I didn't give him the chance. I slammed into him hard enough to move him several inches up the bed with a loud cry. He fisted the sheets, arched his back, and turned his head to the side. He was smiling.

"That's it, baby—fuck me."

I leaned over him, pinning him with my weight, and wrapped my right arm around his neck. My shoulder ached from the action, but I could bear it. This would be over soon. I tightened the choke as I fucked into him, reveling in the feel of him shoving up to meet my thrusts. My skin prickled, and I felt myself racing toward the edge with no hope of stopping.

My teeth scraped along Remy's jaw before I bit down on his lobe hard enough for him to gasp. "Mine," I growled moments before Remy shouted and clenched around me with the rhythm of his body's spasms.

The added pressure and the pleasure of seeing my love so overcome and blissed out pushed me over the edge. My whole body ignited, and I shook with the force of it. I emptied everything I had into Remy through gritted teeth and twitching limbs.

When the last of the aftershocks ceased, I eased my grip on Remy's throat and peppered his cheek and temple in feather-light kisses, uncaring that his hair was plastered to his forehead with sweat. Still inside him, I began to move back, only to be stopped by his trembling hand on my thigh.

"Wait. Just another minute, okay?"

I kissed the back of his neck and smoothed a hand over his glistening back. "Are you okay?"

He hummed. "Understatement of the year."

A smile tugged at my lips, and I kissed between his shoulder blades and anywhere else I could reach. My cock had softened and slipped out of him, and Remy whined, as if he mourned the loss of me inside him.

I fell onto my back next to him, then pulled him into my embrace. He rested his head on my chest and lazily traced his fingers through the hair there. Our hurried breathing evened out without either of us daring to break the silence. There was a lot I wanted to say, though one subject gnawed at me the most. I rubbed my hand up and down Remy's spine, trying to find the right words to explain my actions, or at the very least apologize.

"I can hear your heart beating," he repeated my own words back to me with a playful lilt. "Pretty sure I know why you're panicking." He paused—I didn't take the opening to speak. "You fucked me without a condom, and without us talking about it first."

"I'm sorry. I wasn't thinking."

"You were. Just not about the present. We've never once used condoms in the past. There's a reason I didn't stop you, Max. I knew you wouldn't endanger me in any way, nor would you fuck me without telling me you had something." He said it so matter-of-factly, without a hint of worry.

"I should have said something."

"Yeah? And what about me? The onus is on us both. I didn't volunteer that I'm on PrEP. My point is, we were both caught up and acted kinda..."

"Foolishly," I finished.

"Nah, not quite. We didn't talk about it because it was implied. How many times have I asked you if you still trusted me? That goes both ways, Max. I don't want you feeling guilty about this—not after how fucking mind-blowing it was." He gazed up at me with wonder in his eyes, then he brushed his thumb over my scar. "God, you're so fucking gorgeous."

I hummed to let him know I heard him. Inside, I couldn't help but realize that I was wrong before; I never had a choice with Remy. I'd always been and always would be consumed by his flames.

ELEVEN

REMY

I FEARED THINGS BETWEEN me and Maxim might have become strained after we had sex; no such thing happened. The only source of tension came from me scolding him after I found he'd hurt his shoulder while choking me. Instead of doing the responsible, adult thing and taking sex off the table, I added a rule for it: he had to wear a sling or brace for the next two weeks for the act. Like I said before, I wasn't a fuckin' saint.

The result has been me riding him, or him bending me over a piece of furniture and fucking me until I can't stand. I didn't exactly have much to complain about in that department. We acted like we were making up for lost time, and it was fuckin' great. If I ignored the last decade and the mess I'd become, I could almost pretend that Maxim and I could do this again. I knew he wanted it, no matter how much he tried to hide it—which really wasn't much lately. I didn't think he realized how easily he'd slipped back into that old role. As easy as it seemed, I never let myself forget that it was temporary.

Along with gym visits, we included a trip to Ricobene's at

least once a week in our plans, which was better than VIP Coachella and Christmas combined. Speaking of, the latter was mere days away. We'd already agreed to spend it much like we did Thanksgiving—only with Chinese takeout. Maxim and Roz had also persuaded me to go see my parents.

To say that I was dreading it would be an egregious understatement. We were living in a bubble—in our own little self-contained world. It was perfect, but it was temporary. In a few short months, Maxim wouldn't need me around anymore. The allure of fucking and binge-watching TV shows with his worthless ex would lose its appeal, and then we'd be done. The alternative was worse; if he still wanted me, I'd have to say no. The best outcome would be seeing Maxim get better, and move on. I'd accepted that I was too selfish to stay away from him in the meantime, which only further enforced that I needed to leave before I ruined him for good.

Seeing my parents was another step toward bursting that bubble.

Roz had to work and thus wouldn't be home to serve as a buffer. Maxim had offered, but I wouldn't do that to him; my parents blamed him for the failures in my life, after all. I had an hour and a half to plaster on a smile when my Uber pulled up to the front gates of my family's Barrington Hills estate. It wasn't enough time. I hopped out of the car and opted to climb the fucking gate instead of using the intercom. The few minutes it'd take to walk up the ridiculously long tree-lined driveway would have to give me enough extra time to calm my thoughts.

I sent Maxim a text before I'd gotten out of the car to let him know I'd arrived safely and hadn't bribed the driver to sink us in Lake Michigan. The thought had crossed my mind. As snow crunched under my boots and the wind from the lake didn't chill me to the bone, I was once again grateful for Maxim's kindness and generosity. He'd bought me some other clothes as well, stating that I couldn't live in his pajamas and two outfits. I'd expected my pride or some manly bullshit in me to revolt, but it hadn't happened. I figured the whore in me was stronger.

I was far too used to getting everything from others. I went from my parents, to my friends, to sponsors, then Stan. *And now Maxim.* He wasn't like the rest, and I felt shitty for letting my mind go there—even for a moment. Maxim cared about *me*. He didn't give a shit about my image or what I could do for him, which, honestly, wasn't much.

I had a defined role with everyone else in my life. For my parents, I was supposed to be a good son—one that didn't publicly embarrass or tarnish the family name. I'd failed at that. My friends expected me to be reckless and fun. I'd kept that act up long enough to gain followers, though the people closest to me figured out what a sad, vapid piece of shit I truly was. And my sponsors? Guess you could say I'd let them down the most. People like me were the reason why contracts for public figures—or the dreaded "influencer"—had morality clauses. One hint of a scandal and you're fuckin' done.

Before I could muster the fucks to give for how I'd let Stan down, I was standing on the cleared-off porch of my "home." It hadn't ever felt like it, though. That shitty little studio apartment with Maxim was my only real home.

As I contemplated turning around and running back down the driveway, my phone buzzed in my pocket. I took my gloves off, then fished it out and grinned like a fool when I saw a new message from Maxim.

M: Have you gone in yet?
R: … how'd u kno?

It was a stupid question, but I needed the distraction.

M: I know you. It's been a long time.

M: And your parents can be a lot to take.

R: my dad isn't home. Roz said he was on a trip

M: Go inside, love. It's cold out. Call or text if you need me.

R: I can think of a few ways u can warm me up 2nite

I used the eggplant and winking emojis in case I wasn't being cringy enough already with that reply.

M: Go see your mom. There will be a box of fresh sweets waiting here for you.

M: Then maybe I'll give you some dessert.

Maxim's attempt at sexting left me both snickering and wickedly excited.

R: sounds fuckin perfect

I pocketed my phone and rang the bell.

My mother's shocked expression at seeing me lasted well past what I'd consider awkward. She eyed me from the couch adjacent to the floral linen armchair I sat in. She'd been pleasant enough when she greeted me, though she was staring at me like I was a stranger. In a way, I supposed I was.

She was exactly the same as the last time I'd seen her. Light brown hair trimmed just above her shoulders, blue eyes that held the same coldness that mine and Roz's could, and no wrinkles around her eyes. I doubted she'd had Botox; my mother just never genuinely smiled. For as long as I could remember, I'd never seen her truly happy. My dad wasn't any better.

There she sat, in a designer pantsuit without a single thread or hair out of place, watching me with that fake-as-fuck smile. *Fuuuuck,* I wanted to leave.

"It's such a shock to see you, Remington."

I tried extremely hard not to roll my eyes. "Yeah, you said that at the door."

"Forgive me for being surprised. I haven't seen you in ten years, and then only heard from you when you needed help from William."

William being the family attorney. I might have been cut off financially, but Bill was left available to me to keep the family name out of the mud. After all, I was a Kincaid above all else, and that was what mattered most. *Puke.*

"I've been busy." I sat back and my knee began to bounce.

"It would seem so." Her voice was flat, like she wasn't at all affected by my presence. And I knew she wasn't. It was that apathy that slowly killed me when I was younger. That was part of why I'd loved Maxim so fucking much. He saw me, and he never wanted me to be anything I wasn't.

My attention shifted from my mom's indifferent expression to the immaculately decorated house. Tasteful and elegant Christmas decorations were sprinkled among brand-new furniture in a house that didn't seem lived in. It looked like a staged home, and in a lot of ways it was. Anyone looking in would have seen a perfect family and a perfect home. But perfection was a fucking farce.

"Sit up and stop bouncing your knee. Those habits are unbecoming, and you should know better, Remington."

I flicked my attention back to her and stilled my knee on reflex. I deliberately didn't sit up straight.

"Why have you come today? Do you need something?"

"No. I guess I don't."

For a fraction of a second her eyes narrowed on me. "Did you come here looking for money? Your father and I have already—"

"This isn't about your damn money," I replied, with more irritation than I liked.

"What is it you want then?"

I don't fucking know. "I thought it would be a good idea to catch up. Like you said, it's been so long. I kind of missed my family. I've been seeing Roz a bit," I said with a small, tentative smile. It was then that I knew without a doubt that this had been a stupid idea. Her face didn't soften one bit—she didn't react at all.

"You've been to see Rosalind? She cut off all of her beautiful hair and dyed it much like yours. It's rather garish and unfit for a medical professional."

"That's your takeaway from what I just said? Un-fucking-believable," I muttered.

"Remington—language," she scolded.

"Of course that's what you choose to focus on." I sprung to my feet and strode over to the mantel, which was devoid of any photos.

"You're being awfully dramatic, Remington."

"Will you please stop calling me that?" I snapped.

"I'll have to ask you to leave if you're going to continue to be contrary. I'm expecting company, and your foul attitude is not appreciated."

I tapped my fingers on the mantel, then nodded and spun around to face her. "No need. I'm leaving. It was nice seeing you, Mom," I said as I breezed past her and headed for the hall closet to get my shoes and coat.

She didn't follow or say a word.

"JESUS, YOU'RE FROZEN," Maxim said after he'd unzipped my coat and pulled me into his big, strong embrace.

My teeth were chattering and shivers wracked my entire body. I'd booked a ride back to Maxim's after I'd walked a few miles to a gas station. The ride back had warmed me up, but Maxim wasn't home when I got back. I'd waited outside for him for nearly an hour.

"I'm fine."

"You're not fine. Why didn't you tell me you were coming back so soon?" He rubbed his hands up and down my back and arms.

"She wasn't happy to see me. I'd half been expecting it, but to actually see and hear the indifference in her... I—"

"I'm sorry, love. I'm so sorry. I should have come with you."

I shrugged. "There isn't anything you could have done."

He grabbed my chin and tipped my head back so our eyes met. "Being there would have been enough."

"You're here now." I closed my eyes and buried my face in his chest.

"Let's go take a hot shower—you'll feel so much better after."

He started to pull away, and I clung tighter. "Just stay like this a bit longer."

Maxim grunted then resumed rubbing my chilled back.

"I acted like a fucking child. I literally threw a fucking hissy fit and stomped out of the house. The best part is that I was actually hurt when she didn't try to stop me. Ten years, and she acted like I was a fuckin' stranger." My shivering somehow got worse, and Maxim was holding me tighter. Then I heard a raw, awful sob, and I realized that I wasn't shivering.

Maxim picked me up and carried me over to the couch where he sat us down with me cradled in his lap. I hid my face in his neck, too embarrassed to look him in the eye and see what I might find there. I'd shatter if he pitied me and saw me as weak—even if it was what I was.

I stayed in Maxim's arms long after the worst of my tears ceased, until the only sounds in the apartment were those of our mingled breathing.

"Are you feeling better, love?"

"A bit." I sniffled, not wanting to get his sweater all snotty and worse than I'd already made it.

I heard Maxim swallow, and it made me feel better to know he was nervous. "Do you want to talk about it more?"

"Fuck no."

He let out an amused hum. "Okay. Are you ready for that shower now?"

"This is cozy. Wanna stay like this." Once the fog in my mind cleared more, I remembered something else that had bothered me about the day. I wasn't sure if I should mention it so soon after saying I didn't want to talk, but fuck it. "I realized something today."

Maxim hummed again, the vibration from it comforting me.

"I don't want to end up like them—my parents, I mean. Rich, cold people devoid of any life or redeeming human qualities. I could have easily been like that, you know? Just some rich fucking asshole who doesn't give a shit."

"You're not like that at all."

"But I could have been. I think that's why I let Mac get under my skin so much. He sees me and sees everything I hate in myself. I know he's not really a bad guy. He's annoying, sure, but he's not unjustified in the things he says about me. I get so angry because I agree, and I hate it."

Maxim sighed, and didn't offer any platitudes, which I was thankful for. I hadn't admitted that so he could tell me how great I was or some shit.

"I have something for you. The timing is awful, but I can't wait any longer," Maxim said in a rush.

"Yeah, I saw the lovely turquoise box earlier when you walked up. Thanks for that, by the way."

He shook his head. "It's not that." One of his hands left my back, and a chill replaced it. Maxim pulled something out of his pocket and placed it in my hand. I didn't have to look to know what it was. "I was going to give it to you on Christmas Eve. I-I know we said no gifts, and I'm sorry. It's something I want you to have. Frankly, I should have given you a key last month."

I turned the key around in my palm as the smile on my face grew wider. "Thank you, Max," I replied. A yawn caught on his name and he chuckled quietly.

"You're welcome. *Now* it's shower time, and I'm not taking no for an answer."

As exhausted as I was, my body responded to the sight of a wet, naked Maxim. That of course led to a physical response from him, and our innocent shower turned into something that looked awfully pornographic. Not that I minded one bit.

To my surprise, Maxim never directly touched my cock. Yet he had me on the edge by the time we'd finished from light caresses and well-placed kisses on my neck. His fingers glided down my sides from my ribs to my thighs, sending shivers through my whole body. His short stubble scraped my nape while his hot breath tickled my ear, and his hard cock pressed against my ass and lower back. When I'd tried to push back against him, his hands had held me still, and he continued lavishing me in all the indulgent touches he wanted. I'd nearly melted when he added soap to the mix.

After the teasing shower from Hell—or Heaven, it was debatable—Maxim led me to his room and finally touched me where I'd needed it most. He climbed into bed, then pulled me against his chest facing away from him. Maxim's fingers were cool and slick when they pushed inside me, though the pleasure that came from him massaging my prostate quickly pushed any discomfort to the side.

Unlike the first few urgent times when it was a mad dash to see how fast and hard he could fuck me, he took his time tonight. Probing fingers stretched me while he kissed my neck and shoulder and whispered how much he wanted me. He paid extra attention to the roses on my back as his fingers worked me over. I felt so fucking loved and cherished that I'd almost cried again.

When he withdrew his fingers, I whimpered at the loss of him. He slipped his fingers into my mouth as he held my hip and gradually slid into me. The stretch and burn were *sublime*. Pure fucking ecstasy. Maxim's cock felt like it was burning me up from the inside, and I yearned for it.

I'd always hated the term "making love," but there was no other way to describe what Maxim did to me—what he did for me. He was making love to me, and it was everything I hadn't known I'd needed.

CHRISTMAS WAS every bit relaxing as I'd hoped it would be. We'd spent the day watching movies, eating food, and seeing how many times we could get each other off. I won that competition, but it's not as if either of us truly lost.

The days leading up to the New Year held very much the same, only with less food, and more workouts that didn't take place in the bedroom. Or the couch. Or up against the wall. With regular ice and heat presses, Maxim was able to cut out his painkillers entirely. He'd been on a significantly reduced dose for a couple of weeks but stopped just after

Christmas. I'd had to stop him from flushing the remainder down the toilet, just in case. I couldn't trust him not to get some kind of sex-related injury and need them again.

On New Year's Eve, I finally got to see Eat Cake in person. It was closed to the general public for a private party of Bryan and Elijah's closest friends. I felt weird about going until Bryan had personally invited me at the gym the other day. He'd seemed genuine about it, and I couldn't say no.

The blinds were closed when we walked up, though we could hear music and laughter inside. Maxim sent someone a quick text, and an adorable brunet around my height opened the door a few beats later. I vaguely remembered him from the hospital.

"Hi, Maxim, sorry for making you wait." His gaze traveled to me, and he smiled. "You must be Remy. I'm Eli. Bryan's told me a bit about you, but it's nice to finally meet you. You can't really tell about a person until you meet them, and oh my God, I'm so sorry. Please come in." He stepped aside as a flush colored his pale cheeks. "I talk too much sometimes. Can I take your coats?"

We handed off our jackets to Eli, and he disappeared through a door at the back of the room. I tugged on Maxim's dress shirt and he leaned down so I could speak in his ear.

"He's fucking adorable. Bryan must feel like the Big Bad Wolf around him."

Maxim snorted. "They're perfect for each other. Bryan has the patience of a saint, and Elijah is a great man. He's just nervous with the crowd. And you're new." He tilted my head up for a quick kiss. "Find him one-on-one later, and you'll see a different side of him."

I opened my mouth to reply, then caught frenzied movement coming our way from the corner of my eye.

"Maxim!" a young man shouted as he launched himself at Max and hugged him around the waist.

"Hi, Axel."

"Fuckin' hell, man—I thought you were dead when Bryan called." He said something else in Spanish that I couldn't follow. I knew basic Spanish at best from living in California for years, though this kid was speaking way too fast and it was too loud for me to follow.

Maxim seemed to understand just fine. He smiled and patted the guy on the head in a gesture that made me more than a little jealous.

"I'm fine," Maxim answered. A bunch of other guys, including a *very* handsome Latino guy with sinful brown eyes who gave me an obvious once-over, came over and gave their well-wishes to Maxim. He'd introduced me to each of them, and I smiled and nodded, despite knowing I'd never remember all of those names. Santiago turned out to be my handsome admirer, though he'd cut the flirty glances after one stern look from Maxim. These were his baseball friends, I'd gathered.

Maxim wasn't a big sports guy, I even less. The kind of camaraderie these guys displayed was foreign to me. It was nice to see that Maxim had so many people in his life who cared about him. There were no fake smiles and empty well-wishes being tossed around. These guys really cared, and I could tell that it had bothered them to keep their distance. Bryan and Mac had made that call, and I had to agree that it was the right one until now. Maxim wouldn't have wanted all this attention while he wasn't in full control.

I spotted Eli alone across the room leaning against an exposed brick wall. I gave Maxim a nudge to let him know I was leaving before heading toward Eli. I hadn't noticed Mac or Bryan yet, but I was sure they weren't far.

"Bro, you shaved! You look awesome!" Axel's voice cut above the chatter in the bakery. I chuckled to myself and went over to Eli.

"Hey, again. I wanted to properly introduce myself," I said, holding a hand out to Eli.

"Hey," he replied as he shook my hand. "I'm really sorry about making you guys stand out in the cold earlier. I ramble when I get nervous."

"No worries, man. This is a really nice place."

He perked up at that. "Yeah? I love it in here. It's one of my favorite projects I've worked on."

"What do you do?"

"Advertising and some design. The interior was all Bryan; I just helped get the word out and get people through the door."

"Do I hear a certain someone selling themselves short again?" Mac came up behind Eli and slung his arm around his shoulders. Bryan was right behind them. "This guy also designed the sign and helps Bry with the menu. He also keeps him from being a moody ass all the time," Mac whispered loudly.

Eli and I laughed while Bryan rolled his eyes and cleared his throat. "I can hear you."

"Yeah, I know you can, dude. Doesn't make it any less true."

Bryan pried Mac's arm off of Eli and hauled the obnoxious blond away with him. "Stop harassing my fiancé and come help me get Axe off of poor Maxim."

I talked with Eli more about other projects he'd worked on and learned that he and Bryan had a pit bull that I couldn't wait to meet. Eli was a completely different person when he spoke about her.

When the conversation had shifted to me gushing about the confections, and him telling me about new flavor ideas, another guy joined us. His wavy red hair and piercing blue eyes set him apart from everyone else in the room. I'd seen him with Mac around the hospital, though I wouldn't have guessed they were a thing had Maxim not told me.

"You must be what's got Mac rippin' around at home. I'm Dubhlainn."

"Remy," I replied with a nod. "Has he, ah, said what's got him so riled up?"

He scoffed and grinned. "Knowing him he's jealous that 'his Maxy' has someone new to play with."

"Guilty. Sorry about that, man."

"No bother. It's been fuckin' class watching him mope around and mutter under his breath while he texts Bryan. He's the biggest eejit sometimes, but he's my fella." I heard warmth in his voice.

"Why is Mac upset?" Eli asked with a furrowed brow. "Bryan hasn't said anything about it."

I shrugged and went for nonchalance. "He doesn't like me much. It's nothing big."

The three of us carried on with others coming and going every so often. The longer I talked with Eli and Dubhlainn, the more I relaxed. No one here was treating me like I was this asshole who wasn't welcome. I was… shocked.

I was on my way back to Maxim when I bumped into Mac. To say he cornered me would be more accurate. His jaw ticked while he studied me, but he wasn't yelling or hurling insults, so I held back as well.

"Um, your boyfriend is nice," I offered awkwardly.

"Yeah, Dove's great." The silence between us resumed while we both stood there looking at each other. It was weird. Mac finally sighed and crossed his arms. "Maxim looks good. Better, I mean."

"His shoulder is healing up all right."

"I wasn't talking about his shoulder. He looks happier. I still think you're a dick, but I'm good as long as he's happy."

There was a clear warning in his words, though his casual

delivery softened it. "I've already told you that hurting him isn't my intention."

"What is? Nope, never mind. That's none of my business. How about we keep it that way, with you not hurting Maxim, and I'll try to stop being angry with you over ancient history."

"Sounds good."

"Fantastic," he replied. "Scowling at you is gonna give me premature wrinkles."

I could have let that be that and walked away, but since Mac and I were having a moment of sorts, there was something else I wanted to get off my chest. "Thanks for not bashing me to everyone here. I was surprised no one had any reservations talking to me tonight."

Mac's face twisted up at that. "Why the hell would I do that? They're adults and can form their own opinions. Seriously, what the fuck, dude?"

"*Really?* I had absolutely no reason to worry about it? Asshole."

"Douche."

He cracked a smile, and I couldn't help but do the same. I hadn't realized how childish we sounded before. No wonder Maxim found it more amusing than anything.

"So, what? Are we gonna fuckin' hug it out now or something?"

"Watch it, Remington Steele," he quipped and poked me in the shoulder with two fingers. "Go save Maxim. Bryan and I were only able to keep the Axe-Man away for a few minutes." With that, he left, and I set my sights on the only guy in the room who mattered.

TWELVE

MAXIM

"T HAT KID REALLY LIKES YOU, huh?" Remy asked with a wry smile.

I shrugged. "Axel likes everyone."

"I didn't see him hanging off of everyone."

That couldn't be jealousy tinging Remy's words. Why would he be? "He hasn't seen me in a while, that's all."

He huffed. "If you insist."

"When did you find this little escape?" Remy had dragged us to a small supply closet off of the kitchen after he'd made up an excuse for Axel and the guys. Apparently, he'd needed help finding the restroom.

"I passed Bryan on my way to you and asked if there was somewhere private I could take you."

"That... sounds suggestive."

He raised a brow and cocked his head toward me. "Is that so? I promise I had the purest of intentions, but I'd love to scuff up the knees on these new jeans."

Nope. I didn't give the thought enough traction to visualize it. There was absolutely no way we were doing *that* here.

I shook my head and counted backward from one thousand in multiples of seven for a distraction.

"Aw, come on." Remy pushed off of the shelf he was leaning against and stepped between my legs. "You don't want me?"

"Nine hundred fifty-eight," I mumbled with my eyes closed.

His arms wrapped around my waist and pulled me flush against him. It was impossible to miss the press of his hard cock against my thigh. *Nine hundred thirty-seven.*

"One last chance, Max. Say the word and I'm yours."

I opened my eyes, and he was grinning at me like a fool. "You're a bastard."

Remy broke into a full body laugh that shook his shoulders while I clenched my teeth and tried not to smile too much. "I'm sorry, babe. I'm only fucking with you. I know you'd never want to disrespect your friends like that."

"You really sold it with the hard-on," I said as I slumped back against the door, more than a little relieved.

"Yeah, well, that just kinda happened. I saw the opportunity and rolled with it. What was that nine hundred thing you said?"

"I was counting backwards from one thousand to stop myself from thinking about... what you were proposing." God, it sounded so ridiculous aloud. My cheeks grew warm thinking about it.

"You're adorable. So fucking adorable." He rose up on his toes and kissed me chastely, then dropped back down and returned to leaning against the shelf full of cleaning supplies. "There was something I did want to say to you."

My head perked up, and I watched him scratch the raven tattoo on his neck.

"Thanks for not letting me bail on tonight. I got a little

antsy before we left, but I'm glad I came. It's kinda nice—really nice actually. No one here knows me, and they seem like really good people." Despite his words, Remy looked almost sad.

"Did something happen?"

"No, I mean it. You have great friends. I, ah, came to an understanding of sorts with Mac. I wouldn't say we'll be best buds or anything, but I don't have to worry about him knocking me out either."

That made me chuckle. "He never would have done that. I'm glad to hear—"

I was cut off by muffled voices yelling, counting down from ten. I locked eyes with Remy, and he rolled his shoulders and tipped his head back.

"Come get me."

In two strides I was on him. I hoisted him up and stepped away from the shelf. What was physical strength for if not to impress your lover occasionally?

Lover. Was Remy really my lover now?

Before I could think too much about it, he wrapped one hand around the back of my neck and cupped my cheek with the other. He leaned down to kiss me as the count reached one, then cheers and clapping erupted followed by the distinct pops from bottles of champagne.

"Happy New Year, Max."

"Happy New Year."

Remy grinned, then nipped the tip of my nose before placing a quick kiss on my scar. "Let's go get some bubbly before everyone thinks you fucked the shit out of me in here."

I groaned and set Remy down; there wouldn't be anything I could say to convince Macalister that that *hadn't* happened.

January flew by way too fast. Remy and I had a comfortable rhythm, and I was getting stronger every week. My doctor and physical therapist gave me the okay to start light weightlifting with my right arm, which I couldn't have been happier about. I'd lost enough muscle mass in my arm to have it be noticeable, especially when I was shirtless. Regaining that body symmetry was high on my list of priorities, and I was committed to doing it safely.

Besides, Remy wouldn't let me reinjure myself, no matter how much better the sex would be once my shoulder was back at one hundred percent. In two more months I'd be able to resume my pre-surgery routine. Another month or two after that—and a cleaner diet than what I'd been eating with Rem—and I should be perfect. Almost.

I ghosted my fingers over my scar as I stared at my reflection in a mirror in the gym locker room. Remy had insisted I stay clean shaven and had more often than not been the one to shave me. I couldn't say it wasn't a highly arousing experience, but it also terrified me. Anytime Remy paid close attention to my face, it unnerved me. That was multiplied exponentially when he sat in my lap and shaved my face. There was no way he couldn't see that mar—*everyone* could see it now—and knowing that overwhelmed me at times.

Remy somehow always knew, and he did his best to take my mind off of it. But he wasn't always around. Right now, for instance. He was visiting his sister and there I was, studying my scar, growing more insecure with every passing second.

I had two listings saved that I'd planned on looking at today while I was alone, though all I wanted now was to go home and hide.

I was still slicing carrots into stars for Remy's favorite dish when I heard the lock on the door turn. The thuds from his heavy boots being toed off followed immediately after the door closed and was locked behind him.

"Maxim? Are you here?"

"Kitchen," I replied conversationally. The apartment was silent aside from me chopping vegetables. The rice had already been cooked and was now cooling to make it easier to fry later.

Remy entered the kitchen then flipped on the light. "Hey. What're you doing in the dark?"

"What?"

"All of the lights in the apartment are off. I only guessed you might be here because I could smell food."

Huh. I looked around while I searched for an answer. I couldn't exactly say I hadn't noticed the dark because I was languishing over something I rationally knew was just a scar. Many people had them, yet mine was so much more than just a scar. It was the source of my insecurity and fear, and having it on display made me feel like I was drowning sometimes.

I couldn't fix it, and now I couldn't hide it.

"There's light from the window," I managed to say.

"It's been cloudy as shit all day, Max. Are you okay?" His forehead was creased in concern, and I hated that I'd caused him to worry.

"It's nothing important. I went to the store after the gym, and I'm just tired. I'm making your favorite." I looked and now that the light was on, noticed that some of my stars were crooked. I set the paring knife down and hummed as I picked up the worst of the lot. "Maybe it was a bit dark."

"So you did—go to the store, I mean," he said wistfully.

He crossed his arms and his gaze lowered from mine. "Your rehabilitation has been coming along right on schedule."

I nodded, unsure where he was going with this.

"You don't really need my help anymore."

"What?"

Remy still wouldn't look up and meet my gaze. "I mean, your shoulder is healed enough for you to do just about everything on your own now. You don't need me."

"Of course I do."

"No, you don't. Truthfully, you haven't since the sling came off. All I've been doing since then is costing you money, and—"

"Remy, stop. I don't want you around just because you're helping me—you have to know that."

He shrugged as if he didn't believe me, and I felt like I'd been struck in the solar plexus. Had I not shown him how much he meant to me?

"I've wanted you here because I love you. I always have, and I always will. I want you to stay here with me, not because I need your help, but because I need *you.*"

He flinched at that and looked pained. It dawned on me then that we might not want the same things. Remy had told me we couldn't go back to the way our relationship was, and I'd told him I understood. What if he didn't want to stay? Remy was having some money problems, and surely being here with me—away from his actual life—wasn't helping. I wanted him to stay, but I hadn't considered that he might want to go back to his home. As much as I wished that to be here with me, perhaps it wasn't.

I deflated, shrinking back against the counter. "Unless you want to go back to your life. I'm sorry for not considering that. I know you said you didn't want to us to be like we were, but I'd hoped you might change your mind. I shouldn't have assumed."

"Shit," he mumbled. "Fuck, fuck, fuck! Max, please listen to me. You weren't wrong about us, okay? I don't want…" He reached for me but stopped and pulled back, his gaze dropping. His eyes darted from the floor to me, then back to the floor while his fingers fiddled with a loose piece of thread on his ripped jeans. He looked so broken up, and I ached to ease his mind, but I had to be careful. Remy could run, and who knew if I'd ever see him again this time.

With my own issues pushed aside, I tried to sound calm and collected before the conflicted man just out of arm's reach. "What don't you want?"

Remy shook his head and his foot began to tap. "I haven't been honest with you."

"I know."

"About a lot of things."

I grabbed a dishcloth hanging from the stove behind me and wiped my hands. "Let's go sit down, Rem."

He nodded and let me lead him to the couch where we sat facing each other. Remy sat with one leg folded under him and the other on the floor. His knee bounced as soon as his foot touched the laminate.

"I've fuckin' lied about everything," he blurted out.

Ignoring every fiber of my being, I kept my fingers threaded in my lap instead of reaching out for him. Seeing Remy in distress was harder than anything I'd felt for myself. His ticking jaw told me he was contemplating what more to say, so I let him think.

"I don't have anything in LA to go back to. I lost it all months ago because I'm a fucking disaster, Max. Shit," he hissed, chewing on his thumbnail.

I gently pulled his hand away from his mouth and held it in both of mine, rubbing my thumb over the inside of his wrist.

"I didn't lie to you about being on Instagram. I had a

following, and I did have sponsors—more than I needed to maintain my wasteful lifestyle. I partied a lot. Not just booze, but drugs too." He glanced up at me, searching. He'd find no judgment in my eyes. "Nothing too hard—just some coke and X socially. It got out of hand one night at some party for some fucking event. The guy I was with kept giving me bumps, and I—" His voice cracked, and he looked away from me. "I was so fucking wasted, and I let myself be recorded while several guys took turns fucking me. I honestly don't remember a thing from that night, but I've seen the video. The guy I went to the party with fucking set me up. I- I've done enough blow to know how I react. Whatever happened that night wasn't from that."

I inhaled sharply and felt my stomach flip. "You were drugged."

"I think so." His bottom lip quivered, and he chewed it absently while a tear rolled down his cheek. "I know I'm hardly innocent in this scenario, and I should have known better. Trusting him—"

"No. Do not blame yourself for that. Someone drugged you, love. Anything that happened after that wasn't your fault, and it definitely was not consensual."

"I shouldn't have trusted him."

More tears fell, and I couldn't hold back any longer. I scooped Remy up and pulled him into my lap with his back against my chest. I held him tightly in part to convince myself that he was safe. So long as he was mine, I'd never let any harm come to him.

"I'm not the innocent victim, Max. I've done stuff like that before while I was high, and sometimes when I wasn't. It just feels so good to hurt sometimes. I guess that makes me pretty fucked up, huh?" he asked, his tone dripping with bitterness.

"That's different, love. You made a choice those other times. That was taken from you. I know how that feels."

"I know you do, babe." He sniffled and cleared his throat, reining in his emotions. "There's more. The guy I went with was the one who'd recorded me. He blackmailed me for one hundred grand, and I paid him like a fucking fool. The best part is that he posted the video anyway. I called home in a panic to get the lawyer's number as soon as I saw it on Twitter. This asshole only had a few hundred followers, so it wasn't retweeted too many times before it was taken down.

"Enough people saw it, though. About a week later, clips and screenshots started coming in daily. Word finally got to my sponsors, and my contracts were canceled. You know, because I'd breached all of the fucking morality clauses. I couldn't even deny it. My fucking tattoos gave me away." His chest heaved under my arms in a heavy sigh. "I deactivated my account after that. It became nothing but a source of toxicity, and I was already panicking enough about the rest of my life."

I ran my fingers through his silky hair, noting how much the natural light brown roots had grown in since he'd first arrived. It had only been three short months since I'd woken up with him sleeping at my bedside, yet so much had changed in my life.

"Without income I couldn't keep up with my rent. I had some savings, but not much after I paid that fucking bastard. I got evicted and was staying with a friend for a while. Then I was introduced to a man named Stanley."

Remy said the man's name with so much venom. It pained me to think of why; though not as much as I feared the actual explanation would.

He sunk down lower until his head was in my lap and one bent knee was resting against the back of the couch. "He basically owned me. I lived in his house, he bought me whatever I wanted, gave me an allowance, and in return I was his to do with as he pleased. His little rentboy fuck-toy—at my age, can you believe it?" he asked with a sad smile that didn't reach his eyes.

I brushed his hair back from his forehead and continued to stroke it, hoping it'd offer him some comfort. Remy had been through so much more than I'd imagined. So much more than he'd deserved.

"If you're wondering why I didn't come back after the shit hit the fan, you're not alone. I had it in my head that I'd rather be homeless than accept my parents' conditional support. All that bullshit about wanting freedom to make my own mistakes. Then what did I do? I made myself a slave to a rich asshole who only cared about appearances and superficial shit. Sound familiar?" Remy drew a heart around his face with his index fingers. "You're lookin' at the face of hypocrisy."

"Rem—"

"I stole from him too. I'm a liar and a thief."

"Why?"

"I was at his house in Palm Springs when the hospital called. I was… planning on leaving. When I heard you were in an accident, I dropped everything and came here. I had no money of my own, so I stole Stan's AmEx. He canceled it before you were discharged. Oh, he's the one who cut off my phone too."

My hand stilled at that. "You found out at the doctor's office, didn't you? Two months ago."

He closed his eyes and nodded. "I shouldn't have lied to you about any of it. I just didn't know how to admit it to you."

"Why are you telling me now?"

"I hate lying to you, Max." Remy's eyes welled with tears

that refused to fall. "It fucking eats at me, and makes me feel even worse about myself, but that's not the main reason. You deserve better... you make me want to *be* better. I just don't know if I can be. I've spent so long spinning further and further out of control, and I can see the end."

"The end?"

"Never mind that. I'm just rambling now. All I'm trying to say is that I'm not the person you used to know. I'm not the guy who's worthy of your love and affection. That guy has been dead for years. I'm just... whatever the fuck is left."

His lids grew heavy with resignation, and I finally understood how broken the man in my arms was. Just like his favorite jeans, Remy was fraying at the seams. One wrong tug and he felt like he'd unravel. He didn't value himself, and his dealings with family and the people he'd trusted and considered friends had only exacerbated that. He might not even truly believe in my feelings for him, and I couldn't blame him for it.

"Listen to me, love. I meant every word I said to you earlier, and I still do."

He sat up and his eyes widened. "How could you? I just told you that I was a fucking whore on top of already being a dishonest, vapid person with nothing. Fuck, Max, I have *less* than nothing."

"You've been through many terrible things, but that doesn't make you any less deserving of happiness or love. I know you can't see it right now, but I can." I lifted his chin so his eyes met mine. "Of course you've changed some. It's been ten years—I'd be shocked if you hadn't. You're still you, though. You swear too much and have questionable clothing choices."

"If this is supposed to make me feel better, you've missed the fucking mark," he grumbled.

"You have an insatiable sweet tooth and a devil-may-care

attitude that has never stopped getting you into trouble. All of these things about you are true, Rem. Yet you're also compassionate. You can try to hide it from others as much as you want, but I've always seen it. You have a huge heart, and you try to see the good in people. That's why when they let you down it hurts so much more."

Remy shifted uncomfortably, then made to stand. I reached for him, but he was too fast for me to catch. He paced back and forth next to the couch, his wild eyes flitting between me and the door. I wasn't going to let him leave. Not when I now knew that he truly wanted to stay; he just couldn't let himself believe he was worthy.

He craved love and affection—he thrived on it. I needed him to stay so that I could show him those things. I'd give Remy every part of my soul if it would make him happy.

"Don't run," I scraped out, unable to mask the fear in my voice entirely. I slowly rose to my feet, not breaking eye contact with him. "Please stay. Stay with me, love."

"I—" His voice cracked, and he sucked in a sharp breath. "I can't. I have no right."

With my hands held out in front of me and angled to the sides, I approached Remy as if he were a wounded animal. In a way, he was. "Remy," I cooed. "If you can't stay for you, can you do it for me? Just until you're able to do it for yourself."

His entire body froze. I didn't even think he was breathing.

"It's selfish of me to ask, but I'm desperate. I need you," I repeated, hoping he'd hear the honesty in my words. "Please don't leave me again."

Remy nodded, and with all the fight in him gone, he fell to his knees and began sobbing. I was next to him in two steps and knelt in front of him. He looked up at me, then lunged, wrapping his arms tight around my neck while he cried.

"I've got you, love," I whispered again and again in his ear, and he cried harder. Through all of the tears and choked sobs, I kept him close against my chest and vowed to make him happy. I held him like he was the most precious thing in the world, and I would continue to do so with all of my strength until he understood that.

THIRTEEN

REMY

I N THE DAYS FOLLOWING my complete fucking meltdown, Maxim had—understandably—been keeping a close eye on me. He wasn't at all overbearing or controlling, but it was clear he was worried about me. How could he not be after what I'd confessed? During my emotional word vomit I'd almost let it slip that I'd tried to kill myself. Maxim could never know that.

Maxim gave me space when I needed or wanted it, which admittedly wasn't often, but he was even more tactile and affectionate with me. It was like he'd stopped holding back and could finally love me the way he wanted.

Love. He hadn't said it again in the last week. Really, he didn't have to. It was in every touch, every kiss, and every dopey smile he threw my way. Maxim was a lovesick fool, and it was refreshing seeing him act so comfortably again. He didn't even try to hide it from his friends, though he wouldn't confirm anything either. He merely shrugged or grunted whenever Mac asked. I figured that too was for my benefit.

As happy as he seemed in being able to love me freely, there was something I couldn't stop thinking about. That day

I'd come back and found Maxim in the kitchen, something had been bothering him. My fucked-up issues had taken the spotlight that day, and Max seemed fine ever since, but I knew he was hiding something. Perhaps it took a liar to spot one.

Knowing Maxim as well as I did, I knew there weren't many things he'd lie about. There was just one, really: his scar. He was always aware of it, but he used to fixate on it sometimes to the point where he couldn't think about anything else. Though infrequent, it came in waves. He'd withdraw into himself and away from friends, and even from me sometimes.

I had no way to know for sure without asking Mac or Bryan, but I thought it was safe to assume that Maxim didn't have anyone pushing him outside of his limited comfort zone after I'd left. I hadn't asked him, though it wasn't necessary to know he hadn't dated much after I'd left. Sex, sure. Actually letting someone in and loving them? Not a chance.

Maxim let in so few people that I doubted anyone other than Mac had any idea about the scope of his insecurity. To Maxim's credit, he hid it well. That just made it harder for others to help. As much as I wished he'd be honest and tell me the extent of how much the scar bothered him, I couldn't demand he do so. I had less than zero right to demand honesty anyway. Besides, he'd deny that it was as big of an issue as it so very clearly was.

It was early enough to still be dark out, and I'd been awake with a busy mind since Maxim left for the gym about an hour ago. He'd mentioned going early before Bryan had to go to work. He had better sense than to ask me if I was coming along.

Sighing in defeat, I pushed the covers back and got up to go get my MacBook from the living room. I wasn't ready to be up for the day yet, so I climbed back in bed with it and opened up my email. There wasn't anything useful—shocker. Anyone who gave a shit would text or call. These days that list was exclusive to Maxim or Roz. Speaking of, I had an unread iMessage that had to be from Roz. I kept my phone on the nightstand and it hadn't gone off since Maxim had left. I opened the message, and sure enough, it was a meme from Roz.

I opened Tumblr to find an appropriate one to reply with when an inspirational quote about not suffering in silence caught my attention. It reminded me that people didn't always reach out for help with their mental health. It was something I should have realized, considering I was one of those fucking people. It got me thinking more about Maxim, and what he might be going through.

It didn't take much research to find a name for what he was likely experiencing: some degree of body dysmorphic disorder. I wasn't a fucking doctor, but it sounded pretty damn accurate. I'd always known that Maxim hated his scar and that it made him insecure, but the degree to which it could be plaguing him hadn't crossed my mind.

Looking back, I now saw how his preoccupation was more of an obsession, how his shy nature was more like purposeful avoidance, and why he couldn't seem to believe me whenever I'd tell him how gorgeous he was, or in particular, how sexy I thought his scar was. There were other signs that fit, like his interest in fitness and the constant scruff. The more I read, the more I felt for him and chided myself for not taking his concern as seriously as I could have.

I felt a bit better after I read that exposure therapy was one of the methods used to treat the disorder, but I still kicked myself for not recognizing this as something more than just Maxim being Maxim. I was supposed to be the person who knew him better than anyone else, even after all of our time apart. If he'd been suffering through this alone for over a decade… fuck, I couldn't dwell on that.

There wasn't a single fucking thing I could do to change the past. What I could do was try to limit Maxim's dark days going forward, like he did for me. Valentine's Day was in a week, and we'd already agreed to handle it like the last couple of holidays we'd spent together. I had no money, but I'd find a way to surprise him. It wouldn't be much in the grand scheme, though it'd be a start.

I TEXTED Maxim from inside Eat Cake and let him know I was going out for breakfast with my sister. It was a lie, yes, but my intentions were noble. I'd arrived before Bryan finished at the gym, so I ordered an Americano and one donut, instead of the dozen I wanted. A cute blond rang me up, then I took a seat by the front window where I'd be able to see Bryan coming.

His jet-black hair came into view a few minutes after I'd finished my most nutritional breakfast and was considering a second. I drained the last of my drink, jumped up, and tossed the disposable cup into a trash bin when Bryan walked through the door. He greeted his employee with a wide smile, then his pale green eyes shifted to me. *Jeez, he's hot.*

"Remy, hi," he said with clear surprise. "I wasn't expecting to see you here."

"Hey—sorry to just drop in on you."

"No, no, you're welcome any time. Maxim had just said you were…" His voice trailed off and his brow creased before he glanced around at the two other people seated and getting their morning caffeine fixes.

"My sister isn't here. I told Max I was meeting her so he wouldn't suspect anything."

Bryan cocked a brow at that.

"Wow, shit. That sounded sketchy as hell. I just want to surprise him for Valentine's Day. I was hoping to talk to you about maybe showing me how to bake something for him. If you have the time."

Bryan's expression immediately softened and the corner of his mouth quirked. "Of course. I'll help any way I can, man."

Relief flooded me, and my shoulders sagged. "Thank fuck. Rather, thank *you*. I don't know what Maxim has told you about me, but I don't exactly have a lot I can offer him. He's not huge on super sweet things, though he does like a tamer dessert. Maybe something with fruit or nuts... I don't know."

Bryan nodded toward the door that led to the kitchen and storage areas. "Come with me," he said before he headed for the door. I followed him to a small coat closet and watched as he shrugged out of his jacket.

"Two things, Remy. First, Maxim is very tightlipped about your business and what goes on—or doesn't—between the two of you. You probably already know this, but you don't have to worry about him gossiping about your personal affairs. Today was an exception. Mac was snooping on Maxim's phone when your text came through.

"Second, I might not know the details, but I can clearly see that Maxim is happier than he was before your arrival. That's a lot where a guy like him is concerned. He's not into the superficial bullshit that surrounds Valentine's Day. I think your approach is going to make him melt."

"Really?" I asked, hating how unsure I sounded. I knew Maxim. I knew what he liked, yet I found myself questioning everything I did after the other day. I fuckin' hated it.

"God, yes. I don't know him as well as you or Mac, but I'm confident on this."

I sighed and slumped against the doorframe. "Thanks. I'm all fucked up and out of sorts right now. I'm second-guessing everything."

"It's okay. We've all been there. Were you going to take off your jacket?"

It was my turn to furrow my brow. "Why?"

"I have time today to test out a few recipes with you. Once you decide on one, we can arrange for you to come back and bake a fresh one, if you want. Or I can send you home with the instructions and ingredients."

The thought of *me* trying to bake anything as gorgeous as Bryan's desserts solo made me groan. That was drama I didn't need. "If you really don't mind, I'd like to come back to bake a fresh one. Even with directions, I'd find a way to fuck things up."

He smirked and nodded his head to the side. "Fucking up is a rite of passage with cooking and baking. Even now, some new desserts I make are horrendous. It's all part of the journey."

I shimmied my coat down my arms, then handed it to Bryan's outstretched hand. "Thanks again for this."

Bryan clapped me on the shoulder in a friendly gesture that almost made my fucking eyes go glassy. "Don't sweat it. Take off your boots too. What size are your feet?"

"Ten."

"Perfect, you can wear Eli's clogs." He handed me a pair of hideous leather shoes with massive treaded soles. "Don't make that face. They're just for the kitchen. One, to elimi-nate outside dirt, two, so someone doesn't slip and break something, and three, they are literal clouds for your feet. Well, okay, not literally, but they feel amazing."

"You're the boss. I'll warn you in advance that I'm not the most... competent person in a kitchen. I can make basic things and they taste all right, but I'm not that skilled."

Bryan's smile turned cocky, though the dimples under his dark scruff just made him look cute and sweet. "Good thing I'm a badass *pâtissier*."

Trust me, it's a great thing.

FEBRUARY THIRTEENTH WASN'T Valentine's Day, but when you were trying to surprise the guy you were more or less living with, it was fuckin' close enough. Bryan did me a solid and got Maxim out of the apartment for an evening gym sesh. To ensure they'd be gone long enough for me to get everything ready, Bryan had invited that Axel kid from the New Year's party.

He was harmless, yet I still found myself grinding my teeth in jealousy on my way to and from Eat Cake to pick up the cake Bryan and I had made yesterday. With the last of the leftover money from the last time I went out with Roz, I stopped into a flower shop and wandered around all of the other desperate boyfriends and husbands doing their last-minute shopping. I had enough for a small bouquet, but I opted for a single purple calla lily. It was pretty, yet simple, and I thought Maxim would like that. He loved the purple in my neck and back tattoos, so that made choosing the color easy enough. When I left the flower shop, I was feeling pretty damn good about how the evening would go.

With the food all prepped and keeping warm in the oven, I set out to clean and set the table in the living room. We'd be sitting on the couch or floor, but I still wanted it to be nice for Max. I wiped down the table and stashed away the coasters, unopened mail, and remote.

I'd knocked some crumbs on the freshly vacuumed floor, then cursed myself while I vacuumed the floor *again*. Perhaps next time I'd save the fuckin' vacuuming for last. Once I was satisfied that the apartment was sufficiently clean, I went back to the kitchen to grab the calla lily. I unwrapped it then stared at it blankly while it sunk in that I'd forgotten to get something to put it in. Groaning at my oversight, I checked the cupboards for something suitable, and came up empty. No vases, and all of the cups were too wide at the top. The flower just kind of flopped around, and it looked ridiculous. It hadn't occurred to me that a single man in his early thirties might not have flower vases sitting around. *Ugh, dumbass.*

A notification from my phone caught my attention, and I set down the glass and flower on the counter to pull it out. A text from Bryan said Maxim was on his way home, which meant I had about fifteen minutes to finish getting ready. I typed out a quick thanks then pocketed my phone when I noticed a couple of beers next to the fridge. I eyed the narrow necks of the bottles, and had the cap off of one in seconds.

A few chugs of warm beer, thirty seconds of rinsing the bottle and a quick snip to the flower stem, and the lily had a fuckin' vase. Was it classy? Fuck no, though it was kind of cool. I took the bottle out to the table and set it down... on the otherwise empty table. I was missing something fundamental for the romantic dinner—

Candles. How had I forgotten to get candles? A quick glance to the rest of the room revealed that there weren't any candles sitting around—shocker. I checked the time, and still had eleven minutes, so I tore apart the two hall closets. After enough frantic snooping to make me break out in a sweat, I found a goddamn candle and brought it over to the setup on the table. It wasn't a five-star restaurant, but it was the best I could do under the circumstances.

I checked the time again and winced: less than five minutes. I stripped off my clothes, and showered in record time, redressing in sweats and a tee, because that's what was clean and on top of the pile. *So romantic.* I was lighting the candle when Maxim walked in with tired, heavy-lidded eyes that warmed when he saw me.

"Surprise," I said nervously.

"What's all this?" he asked with a devastatingly handsome lopsided grin.

I strode over to him while he dropped his gym bag to the floor, then I threw my arms around his neck. "It's Valentine's Day tomorrow, and I wanted to do something nice for you. I cooked a lot of food, so you'd better fucking be hungry."

He huffed a laugh and squeezed me tight "You're amazing."

My cheeks flushed, and I buried my face in the crook of his neck. "Yeah, wait until you taste supper before you go singing my praises. I'm still a shitty cook."

Supper wasn't anything fancy; I made chicken breasts, rice, and veggies. It was a meal we'd had dozens of times, yet Maxim thanked me as if I'd grilled the perfect Wagyu steak. He also loved the purple lily, and even thought the beer bottle was cute and "so me." As soon as I'd told him to sit down, he'd noticed that I'd cleaned everything. I had to jet off to the kitchen to keep from turning bright red and combusting.

I'd calmed down while we ate and chatted, but now that I was looking down at the cake I'd helped bake, I lost all my fucking chill. Why had I chosen a damn cake at all? Protein bars or something would have been better. *It's fucking nice, though.* Under Bryan's direction I'd decorated the sugar-free, spiced carrot cake with drizzled cream cheese glaze, instead of all-over frosting. Bryan whipped up some pecan crumble thing that went on the cake as well. It certainly wasn't anywhere up to the standard of Bryan's masterpieces, but it tasted good, and it was something I did.

I sucked in a deep breath, then did as Bryan had instructed and brought out the whole cake along with a knife and two forks. He'd said something about slicing it in front of Maxim so he could see the whole thing first. Made sense.

My palms were sweaty, but I managed to not drop the cake, which I took as a small victory. I set it down on the table in front of Max, then dropped to my knees next to him.

"You got a cake too? So romantic," he teased.

"Correction—I baked you a cake. Well, Bryan helped. A lot. He helped a lot, but I decorated it."

His smile turned warm again and he rubbed the back of his neck. "Thank you, love. This is perfect."

"Yeah?" I exhaled a long breath.

He nodded. "What kind of cake is it?"

"Carrot. There are some nuts in it too." I sliced a large piece and pulled it out so he could see. "Have a bite."

Maxim picked one of the forks and scooped off the tip of the slice. His eyes lit up when the cake hit his tongue. "This is fantastic, Rem. It's not too sweet." He took another, bigger bite then hummed. "Thank you for tonight. I already said it, but it's perfect."

"You're welcome. You do so much for me; I wanted to do something nice for you."

"You do a lot for me too."

"It's not the same," I said, shaking my head. "There's a power imbalance between us, yet you don't make me feel…" *Like a whore.* "Like I'm less than or some shit. I can't thank you enough for that."

Maxim set his fork down and nodded again. "You don't have to thank me, but I understand what you're saying, and I appreciate the gesture." He closed the short distance between us and kissed me hungrily, lip biting and all.

Heat flooded me in an instant and incinerated all of the insecurities I'd been plagued with during the last few days.

We hadn't been sexually active since my confession, and I couldn't really explain why. We weren't awkward around each other, and I certainly still wanted him, yet neither of us tried to initiate anything beyond kissing.

I fisted the front of his T-shirt and pulled him closer, needing to feel his solid frame against me. To my delight, Maxim pulled me up into his lap, and I wrapped my legs around his back.

"I don't want to watch TV tonight, love," he panted.

"Fuck the TV." I pressed my lips to his while I rocked my hips, grinding my growing hard-on against his. I loved the feel of that massive cock stretching and filling me until I thought I couldn't take any more, but I had other plans tonight—if Maxim was into it.

I licked into his mouth, pulling out every trick I knew would drive him crazy. His hands tightened on my waist when I nipped his scar, so I did it again.

"Remy," he growled.

I tweaked one of his nipples and bit him again.

He roughly shoved a hand down the back of my pants and squeezed my ass hard enough to bruise. I hissed and rolled my hips harder into his lap, making us both groan. I took the brief break from our kiss to pull his head back and suck on the sensitive skin above his collarbone. I was usually the one between us to bear marks from sex, but I wanted everyone to know that Maxim was fucking mine.

Maxim hissed and pried me off of his neck. I looked at the brutal red mark I'd left with a toothy grin. I could have written "property of Remy" on his forehead in a Sharpie for as subtle as the mark was. "More," I demanded.

"When did you turn into a vampire?"

"Since you started tasting so fucking good." I leaned in for his neck again, but he held me back.

"Behave, Rem. No more marks." His voice was calm yet stern, and it made me melt. Bossy Max was fucking hot.

"Then give me something else to suck on."

He blew out the candle and his already dark eyes turned black. With both hands supporting me, Maxim stood and carried me to the bedroom. To ensure he was riled up enough to be rough with me, I bit his neck hard, just above the other mark. Maxim winced, then set me down in front of the bed instead of tossing me onto it as I'd expected.

"On your back—head toward me. Now."

I did as instructed and hung my head over the edge of the bed. My whole body throbbed in anticipation of what was about to happen as I glanced up at Maxim. His eyes were locked on mine as he pushed his pants down far enough to free his hard cock mere inches from my face. He was fucking hung to begin with, but this angle made it all the more apparent. I'd have doubted I could take him if I hadn't already had firsthand experience in doing so.

Maxim leisurely stroked himself and I licked my lips, hungry for a taste. Watching his foreskin slide over his cockhead was going to drive me in-fucking-sane. I reached for my own cock and squeezed, only to still when Maxim growled.

"Hands on the bed." He traced my parted lips with two fingers before he sank them into my willing mouth. I sucked on them as if they were his gorgeous cock—hoping soon they would be. "Beg for it."

Yeeesss. "Please," I said though it came out muffled around his thick fingers.

"Please what?"

"Please fuck my throat."

His fingers faltered for a moment, and I thought I hadn't pushed him enough. Then his other hand guided his cock to my lips. Instead of giving me what I wanted, he rubbed the blunt head along my cheek, leaving a smear of pre-cum in its wake.

"Don't fucking tease me."

"That isn't begging."

"Please—Fucking *please.*"

His cock twitched in his hand then he brushed the tip against my lips. I couldn't resist and took a swipe at him with my tongue, savoring the taste of him. Maxim jerked back and shivered. I grinned. I opened my mouth to tease him, and he stuffed it full of that gorgeous cock, stopping before he reached my throat.

"No more talking," he ground out, rubbing the corner of my stretched mouth. He pulled almost all the way out, then pushed back in, moving slowly. I closed my eyes and did my best to relax my throat in anticipation of what was coming.

One of Maxim's hands gripped my throat while the other held my head angled back, keeping my throat open. Without any warning, he pushed all the way in until my nose tickled from his pubes. His musky scent was dulled from his earlier shower at the gym, but I loved it all the same.

I moaned, long and needy, around the cock in my mouth, reveling in the glide of it over my tongue. Maxim kept his thrusts slow and measured at first, no doubt to fucking torture me. I wanted him to bruise my throat, and I wasn't above whimpering for it.

"Are you ready to hurt for me again, love?" he asked reverently.

My eyes fluttered closed and I groaned. Maxim brushed his thumb over the hollow of my neck then forced his cock as far as it would go, again and again. The rough, relentless pace brought tears to my eyes, yet I loved it. Maxim's labored breaths were the sexiest sounds and only made my own dick harder.

He fucked my throat raw until I felt him swell and pulse,

coming down my throat. He grunted and mumbled about how perfect I was while he caressed my neck and jaw before slowly pulling out. I caught a small taste of him from one last spasm on my tongue.

"Thanks for dessert." I sat up and made a show of licking my lips. "Come 'ere, big guy."

Maxim joined me on the bed and kissed me gently, belying the ferocity he'd just displayed when he fucked my face. And that was one of the things that made being with Maxim so different—no matter what we did, he still respected me. Even when he used me during sex, I never truly felt like I was being exploited. He would die before he disrespected me.

Sweet kisses were fantastic, but I wasn't done. Using Maxim's weakened state to my advantage, I pinned him on his back, knocking the air out of his lungs. His brows rose in clear surprise, and I grinned wolfishly.

"I'm not remotely finished with you yet." I worked a hand between us and cupped his balls, drawing a sharp gasp from him. "I hope you have more for me. I need another taste." I licked up the side of his neck, then sucked on his earlobe.

Maxim's back arched off of the bed, lifting me as well. When we came back down, I rolled his balls around in my palm and watched him squirm from oversensitivity. I needed him naked, and I fucking needed it now.

"You're wearing too many fucking clothes." He hurriedly took off his shirt while I pulled his pants and boxers down. My own shirt followed, and I shoved my pants down as fast as I could. I was back down on Maxim in seconds, rutting against him as best I could without getting too worked up. The need to come had been building since Maxim first kissed me, but I had to hold off a bit longer.

With Maxim naked and momentarily spent beneath me,

keeping myself in check was going to be fucking hard. He was so responsive to every touch and kiss, and every sound he made went straight to my cock. Starting with his lips, I kissed and teased every inch of him I could get my mouth and hands on. His cock joined the party again while I was lapping at one of his nipples and tweaking the other.

I scooted down until that monster cock was close enough to taste again, then I licked him from balls to tip, smiling when his entire body shuddered. I squeezed his powerful thighs, then sat up and sucked on my index finger. Maxim's head was tilted back so he couldn't see me or anticipate what I was about to do.

His cock twitched and was too damn inviting. I stroked him leisurely with my free hand while I guided my spit-slicked finger between Maxim's legs. He jerked and his eyes shot to mine when I rubbed small circles around his hole.

My hand shifted from his cock to rub his hip. I needed him to relax, and sexual stimulation alone wasn't going to be enough for that. "Relax, babe. Trust me." I pressed harder, sinking the tip of my finger inside him as he sucked in a sharp breath. He tensed and I stilled, waiting for him to calm. I kept rubbing his hip and thigh until his body loosened enough for me to push in deeper.

"I want you, Max. How long has it been for you?" He whimpered in response, whether to my probing finger or the question, I wasn't sure. "That long, huh? Do you remember what it feels like to have me fucking you? Working you apart from the inside until I've drawn every last drop from you? Yeah, you couldn't forget that." My throat was hoarse from the brutal throat-fucking I'd endured, but seeing the reaction my words had on Max was worth the pain of speaking.

He looked wrecked from the mere thought of having me inside him again, which I took as an invitation to press in as far as I could. I found his prostate without any trouble and massaged it, mirroring the motion of my hand on his hip. Maxim's hands fisted the sheets at his sides, and he squirmed, mumbling incoherently.

I leaned down and kissed the head of his leaking cock, then carefully withdrew my finger. "Head up on the pillows, babe." He nodded and did as instructed while I got the lube from the nightstand. I settled back between Maxim's legs and coated my fingers with a few pumps of lube. Maxim hawkeyed me the entire time, which told me I had some work to do before he'd be relaxed enough to take me.

I couldn't say for certain, though I was pretty sure Maxim hadn't bottomed much—if at all—since I'd left. It had taken four years of us being together before he told me he wanted to try it, and I couldn't imagine him trusting someone else enough to do it. Having Maxim surrender control to me was intoxicating, and the feeling was back in full fucking swing now.

Just breathe and focus on his cues. I gave myself a mental shake before turning my full attention back on Maxim. His chest heaved and his forehead was slightly creased; he was nervous and scared. I leaned over him and kissed him while my lubed-up fingers wrapped around his cock.

The kiss was slow and deep, never becoming needy or frantic. We tasted each other like we had all the time in the fucking world, and for that time, it felt like we did. None of the other bullshit mattered when I had Maxim this close. My sole concern was his happiness, and I knew I could succeed at that.

At the time my tongue skimmed over the roof of his mouth, I pressed a finger past the tight ring of muscle fighting to keep me out. He moaned into the kiss, and I pushed more. When I added a second finger, he tore away from my mouth and hissed.

I kissed and licked at his exposed neck and told him to

breathe and relax for me. "I want you so fucking badly. I dream about being inside you and making you mine again." Another finger. "Tell me you want that, Max."

I brushed his prostate, and he whimpered.

"Do you want me to fuck you?"

"Yes," he pleaded on a broken sob. "God, yes, Rem."

I withdrew my fingers and fumbled the bottle of lube. I could have blamed it on my slippery hands, but that wasn't it. My hands were shaking. I balled my fist and took deep breaths to try to calm my nerves. Maxim trusted me, and I had to believe he wouldn't if he thought I'd hurt him.

With that in mind, I slicked up my cock, and rubbed it over his hole while I got in position, kneeling between his legs. I looked up to meet Maxim's gaze, relieved when I saw nothing but want in his eyes. He nodded once, then let his head fall back on a rough sigh as I pushed inside of him.

"Fucking hell, Max," I gritted out. He was so fucking hot and tight. My fingers dug into his thighs and my body tensed while I gave him a chance to adjust to me and willed myself to calm the fuck down.

I shifted my hips back, testing how he'd respond. When I saw him bite his lip and heard the low, sultry moan, I went for it. My hips rocked into him with long, deep thrusts that grazed over his prostate, judging from his wide eyes and vocal reaction. I kept my pace slow yet steady, focusing all of my energy on staving off my orgasm and drawing every last bit of pleasure out of Maxim that I could.

The leftover tension bled out of him, and he was truly mine. I slid my hands down lower, toward his groin, and snapped my hips forward hard enough to cause a loud smack in the otherwise quiet room.

The sound that fell from Maxim's lips had me smiling. Something between a moan and a muffled curse—but not quite. Maxim wasn't the type to curse often, and I'd be eternally proud if I could fuck one out of him. With a new goal in mind, I let go of one of his legs, leaned forward, and grabbed his left shoulder for leverage. I fucked him hard, though not enough to hurt him. He wasn't the little pain slut I had the tendency to be.

Sweat dripped from my nose and hair, mingling with Maxim's on his chest, and I felt exhaustion start to seep into my muscles. I couldn't stop. I wouldn't, even if it killed me— my cardio was bad enough that it might.

Digging deep, I pressed on, every thrust bringing me closer to falling over the edge. Maxim was right there with me. His breathing sped up, and one of his hands went to his cock, stroking it in time with my movements.

"I'm so fucking close," I said, knowing my words would help get him there.

On a series of strangled grunts and sighs, Maxim exploded between us. His hot cum dripped from my chest while his ass clenched around me, taking me over the edge.

I didn't just fall; I fucking ran and dove off headfirst.

My entire body trembled with the force of my orgasm, and I collapsed on Maxim's heaving chest, spent and boneless. "Holy fucking shit."

Maxim rubbed my back in soothing circles, not seeming to mind that I was a sweaty fucking mess. He kissed the top of my head, and I took my initiative to at least get up high enough to kiss him one last time before I expired.

I slowly eased out of him, then crawled over his leg and higher up the bed to rest my head on his shoulder. I stretched, and he met me halfway in a lazy kiss.

"Hi," I said.

"Hi. Did you wash the sheets?"

"Yeah," I rasped, sounding even worse now that I was out of breath.

"Thank you. Are you all right?"

I held up my hand with my index finger and thumb joined in the "a-okay" symbol. "Dying, but okay."

"You're sure I didn't hurt you?" Maxim asked, propping himself up on an elbow.

"I could ask you the same thing, you know."

He narrowed his eyes at me, and I snorted.

"It's a little tender"—I touched my neck—"but I'm fine. I'll let you look at it and feel me up later. I just need to die right now."

Seemingly pleased with that, he picked up my hand, entwined our fingers, then kissed mine. "Thank you for tonight. For all of it. I…" His fingers began to absently trace one of my roses.

My breathing stopped, and I waited for him to finish.

"I love you, Remy."

Relief flooded me, and I fought back the tears that stung my eyes. "I love you too, Max."

No more fucking crying.

FOURTEEN

REMY

WITH VALENTINE'S DAY behind us, I set my sights on the next important day: Maxim's birthday. Thanks to Bryan's help, Valentine's turned out fucking amazing. It was an important day for me and Maxim, and I wanted his birthday to be as well. The weeks since then had been great too. I hadn't caught Maxim being as obsessive over his scar, and a small part of me began to believe that maybe I could stay with Maxim—even if I believed I didn't deserve it.

Nothing significant or world-changing happened, I just felt like it could work from the small, everyday interactions we had. I actually *liked* cooking for him, and I wanted to improve my limited skills. Cleaning wasn't my favorite, but seeing Maxim so happy made the menial work not so bad. I'd never be a fucking Stepford wife, though I was doing better. We were living an ordinary life—one that I imagined we would have had had I never left, and it was *everything*.

As blissfully ordinary and spectacular as it was, our arrangement wasn't without flaws. We both had a knack for not willingly discussing difficult shit, which was how three more lovely weeks had gone by without any talk of what the hell I was doing. Was I living with Max now? It seemed that way—and it sure felt like it—but I knew better than to put stock into an assumption. At least I used to.

My contrary ass didn't seem to mind making assumptions this time. I already knew what Maxim would say too. He saw things in black and white; I was with him now, and I was staying. End of story. My vision was normally gray.

My "normal" hadn't exactly worked out for me, so I was trying it Maxim's way.

In the past, we'd have spent his birthday getting pizza, watching movies, and fucking. That was more or less what we'd been doing during his recovery, so I wanted to give him a different experience. We stuck to that when we were younger because I was all he had. After he'd aged out of foster care, he was on his own, and I was right there with him.

That wasn't the case anymore. Maxim had friends now, some he'd known almost as long as he'd known me. He'd never admit to wanting a party for himself, though I had a feeling it'd make him smile. He might clam up at first if he had to be the center of attention, but if I planned a good party, that wouldn't happen. Given my years of experience doing little else, I was confident in my ability to do just that.

The problem would be getting everyone together and finding a space. I kinda lacked the resources to make that happen solo. I'd reached out to Bryan a few days ago, and he thought the party was a wonderful idea, but he wasn't much of a party planner. As a result, Eli had his hands full with their wedding plans. I felt for the guy.

Bryan had given me an alternative I'd been dreading: Mac. Sure, we'd come to sort of a gentleman's agreement to not be shitty with each other, but we were hardly best buds. I saw him around on the days I accompanied Maxim to the gym, and the few times he'd convinced Maxim to go out for drinks. He still annoyed the ever-loving shit out of me, even if he was an okay guy.

I sat on the closed lid of the toilet with my knee bouncing and my phone in hand, thumb hovering over Mac's designation: Douche. Bryan gave me his number, and I'd tried to think of another way. There wasn't one.

Sighing in defeat, I tapped his name and started typing.

R: Hi, its Remy

The "Read" message appeared immediately, then... nothing. My knee came to a halt and my nerves shifted to rage. That motherfucker was going to leave me on Read?! I muttered curses low enough to not alert Maxim out in the living room and was about to call Mac and tell him to eat my entire fucking ass, when a new message appeared.

D: Jeez. Took you long enough to message me, dude.
R: what?
D: Don't be dumb, fuckboy.
D: Bry told me he gave you my number. Days ago, dude.

Of course he did. Now I felt like a fuckin' idiot.

R: w/e. Did he tell u why I needed ur number?
D: My guy, the shorthand needs to STOP.

I groaned louder than I'd intended to and my knee resumed bouncing. "Asshole."

R: Greetings! Has our mutual comrade informed you of the purpose of my message on this here fine fucking day?
D: Bravo, good sir.
D: That's much more fitting of a guy named Remington.

D: And yes, Bry told me what was up. I'm down to party plan, dude.

R: gr8

I deliberately went back to shorthand in hopes it would piss him off, even just a little.

D: You're gonna be *that* bitch?

I was one hundred percent *that* bitch. I left him on "Read" and counted the seconds in my head before he replied. I made it to thirty-seven.

D: Fine. Be like that.

D: Texting you is exhausting.

D: Get away from Daddy tomorrow and come over. We'll plan this motherfucker, then you can lose my number.

R: works for me

Mac sent his address, then I locked my phone and slid it back into my pocket. I flushed the toilet and ran the tap for my cover before I went back out to the living room to spin another white lie.

"What did I miss?" I asked as I sat down between Maxim's outstretched legs and leaned back against his chest.

"Bonnie is back from the dead."

"Already? By who?" We'd long since caught up on *Supernatural* and were now watching *The Vampire Diaries*. Who knew Maxim would enjoy teen drama so much?

"Don't know yet. I could have paused it when you got up," he grumbled.

He was too fucking adorable when he was grumbly. "I know, but it's so much more fun to ask questions." He snorted a laugh, then pulled me closer and kissed the top of my head. "Hey, do you need me for anything tomorrow morning? I thought I'd go see Roz again, if that's all right." Not the smoothest segue. Fucking sue me.

"I appreciate that you still want to take care of me, but I can make my own breakfast on occasion, love. Go see your sister—you don't have to ask permission."

Had I? Shit, I guess I did. "Right. Thanks."

He hesitated, though I knew he wanted to say more from the change in his breathing. "How much money do you need?"

Shit. I'd forgotten that using Roz as an excuse meant accepting more money from Maxim. I'd been going to visit her more during breaks on her shift and around mealtimes to cut down on taking money from Max. One of those quick visits wouldn't cover me for as long as I'd probably need with Mac. The lie had gone unnoticed for Valentine's Day, but Maxim wasn't distracted now.

"Oh, yeah. Twenty would be great, thanks."

"Can I send it to you? I don't have much cash on hand." He sounded apologetic, and I hated it.

"Sure, babe. I should probably get a job soon, huh? There's gotta be something out there even I'm qualified to do."

Maxim swept the backs of his curled fingers up and down my chest and sighed. "Please don't belittle yourself like that. You'll figure it out in time."

I tilted my head back and waited for him to kiss me, effectively ending the conversation.

He didn't make me wait long.

I PULLED up the address Mac had sent over once more before I knocked on the door at the end of a quiet hallway.

At least it had been quiet when I stepped off of the elevator. The closer I got to the door, the more pronounced the thud of booming bass became. It was muffled through the door, though I recognized the song to be one from Marky Mark. Yeah, I was at the right fucking place.

My knock went unanswered so I hammer-fisted the door like the FBI with a warrant. The music paused, then footsteps grew louder. Mac pulled the door open and greeted me with a wide smile I hadn't expected. The fucker was also only wearing boxer briefs. It was a damn shame a body like that had to be on a guy like him.

"Ah, you didn't get lost," he said teasingly.

"GPS."

"Come on in, lost boy." He stepped aside and opened the door wider, then closed and locked it behind me.

"I didn't get lost."

"Yeah, that's totally not what I meant, but I shouldn't be surprised it went over your head."

A door swung open down the hall, then Dubhlainn stomped into the kitchen and crossed his arms over his chest. His short red hair was a wavy mess, not unlike Mac's blond hair.

"Mornin', Remy. How ya?"

I side-eyed Mac, then smiled at his much more tolerable —and reasonably dressed—boyfriend. "Good, man. Sorry to drop in so early."

"It's no bother. And *you*," he said, directing his attention to Mac. "I told ya to quit actin' like a fuckin' eejit. Behave."

"Yes, Dove," Mac grumbled.

Dubhlainn turned back to me and excused himself to go study in his room. Once the door closed behind him, I cracked a smile and looked over at Mac.

"I get it now. Little red there owns you."

"Shut up."

I held up my hands in front of my chest. "Sure thing. *Bro*."

He shivered and wrinkled his nose. "Ew, you don't get to bro me."

"Whatever. Couldn't you have put some fucking clothes on? You knew I was coming."

His expression went blank and he let his head fall to one side. "In my own place? Really?"

I sighed, not wanting to admit he had a point, but man enough to concede. "Fair. Maybe we can get on with the planning portion of the morning? I can't be gone all day."

Mac snorted and rubbed his scruff. "Does Daddy keep you on a short leash? That doesn't sound like Maxy."

"Fuck you."

"You wish. Sorry not sorry, but you're not my type."

We stood there in the wide-open space behind the couch, glaring at each other like cartoon nemeses. Then my stomach grumbled louder than it had ever fucking done before. In keeping with the lie that I was going out for breakfast, I'd left without eating. I clenched my fist and waited for a joke, but none came.

"Want something to eat?"

"Um. Yeah, sure."

"Come," he said on a sigh, turning around and heading toward the large kitchen. "And try not to check out my ass too much."

Fucker.

He motioned for me to sit at one of the tall stools at the kitchen island, then walked around the counter and went for the fridge. "Bacon and eggs, leftover pizza, or Froot Loops?"

I narrowed my eyes at him, not sure what caused the sudden uptick in hospitality and not fully trusting it. He closed the fridge, crossed his arms, and leaned a hip against the counter.

"Look, I'm sorry about just now. I was being a dick, and it was rude. We made our truce, and I need to remember that. Also, Dove will skin me if I keep being rude to a guest." He waved his hand around absently. "Irish hospitality is apparently a serious thing."

He sounded genuine, and I relaxed a bit. "I wasn't exactly my best either."

"Good. Now that we're past that, what can I get you for breakfast?"

"I'm never gonna turn down bacon."

"Comin' up." He spun around to the fridge and took out a pack of unopened, thick-sliced bacon. Fan-fucking-tastic. Once a non-stick frying pan was lined with meat and the rest was back in the fridge, he stood with his back to me and washed his hands. And I one hundred percent did not check out his ass. Fucking bastard.

"So," he drew out as he dried his hands on a dish towel hanging from the stove, then faced me. "How do you want to do this?"

"I'm not too sure," I replied, scratching at the raven on my neck. "I don't know what you guys usually do, but I thought it'd be kinda cool to throw him a party. Ah, but one where he isn't going to feel like the center of attention—he wouldn't like that."

"Any chance of you telling me why he hates attention? I know he goes to great lengths to avoid it, and I'm pretty sure he knows I know, though he hasn't told me why."

"Not a chance. Maxim isn't the type of man to volunteer that kind of personal information, and I don't think he'd appreciate me gossiping about him."

"You're right. I shouldn't have pried."

I snorted a laugh, despite his defeated tone. "Prying is kinda what you do. You haven't changed much from what I can tell."

"Woooow—thanks for the compliment, dick."

"I wasn't finished, douche," I quipped, biting back a smirk. "You're still the same Macalister that Maxim loves and trusts. He thinks of you like a brother. Still, he's not gonna just tell you his deepest fears and worries over shots at the bar. If you sit him down alone and ask him directly, he'll probably tell you."

Mac got a guilty look on his face and scratched the back of his neck. Before he turned around to poke at the bacon.

"Mac, have you ever tried seriously asking him about it?"

A loud pop and flying grease had Mac hopping back from the stove. "Not really," he said regrettably while he strode over to a hook on the wall by the hallway and grabbed a gray apron. He hooked it around his neck and faced me while he tied it around his back. "I tried a few times when we were younger, and he always shut me down or straight-up lied and said he was fine. Instead of continuing to pry, I accepted he didn't want to talk about it and moved on. I tried my best over the years to be mindful of what I thought his limits were." A heavy sigh fell from his lips. "I guess I've been kind of a shitty friend."

"Nah, not even." I waved that sentiment off with a flick of my wrist. "He adores you, even when you're annoying the shit out of him." That made Mac smile. "You gave him exactly what he thought he needed: some degree of space and his privacy. Most importantly, you fuckin' stayed, and that means more to him than anything."

I swallowed hard and laid my hands flat on the counter. I hadn't meant to say that last part. I couldn't change that I'd left, and I frankly wasn't sure I would've even if I could've. Staying could have ruined us, and I couldn't handle Maxim ever hating me. *Fuck.* I needed to calm down.

Mac noticed my distress yet had the decency not to

comment on it. "He gets all depressed about his birthday—how about we not let that happen this year, yeah?"

"Why is he depressed around his birthday?" I asked like the fucking dumbass I was.

"Why do you think, Remington Steele?"

I hung my head. I didn't have to answer. I'd left the day after Maxim's twenty-second birthday. Before I could take a stroll down memory lane and get the shit kicked out of me, Mac snapped his fingers in front of me.

"Stay with me, dude. What's done is done. Let's make this year epic," he said with a grin.

The blond fucker was right. I couldn't get sucked into all of that negative bullshit again. I switched gears and launched into an idea I had for the party. Mac nodded along and shared my sentiments, and I felt like we were getting somewhere.

"Max's apartment isn't big enough to comfortably fit many people, so I'm not sure how well that'll work."

Mac waved that off. "Don't worry about that. We can have it here. The music will be better too."

I scoffed. "That's debatable. I heard that shit you were listening to when I got here."

"For the love of God, why doesn't anyone want to acknowledge the greatness that is Marky Mark and the Funky Bunch?! 'You Gotta Believe' is an underrated classic."

He launched into an animated run that had me struggling to keep my laughter at bay. I lost the battle when he brought fucking Vanilla Ice into the mix. While my shoulders were still shaking, my phone buzzed from inside my pocket. I fished it out, noted I had a new email, then opened up my mail app. My smile faded when I read Stanley Robson's name at the top of my inbox.

I took a deep breath, then deleted the email. Fuck that

guy. I was done with him, and I couldn't have given two shits about whatever he had to say.

"You good, dude?" Mac asked with a furrowed brow. "Get some bad news or something?"

I pocketed my phone and shook my head. "Nah, it's just annoying spam. You were talking about your shit taste in music, please do carry on."

And he did without missing a beat—much to my amusement. Or regret. It was really a toss-up.

FIFTEEN

MAXIM

REMY WAS UP TO SOMETHING. He thought he was being sneaky, but he really was an awful liar. He'd been spending more time on his phone, smiling and groaning at something. When I'd inquire, he'd lock his screen, pocket his phone, and say some variation of "nothing, just a stupid meme."

I had a fairly good idea that it was regarding my upcoming birthday on the eleventh, and that eased any would-be tension around the deception. I'd never fault Remy for wanting to surprise me, though I was very curious to see what he was plotting, and with whom.

To let him have his surprise, I didn't try to figure out what he was up to, and I played oblivious. Remy's meetings with his "sister" increased and lasted longer, and I found myself at a loss for what to do at home. For the first time in my adult life since Remy had left, I felt alone. So much so that I couldn't fathom how I'd spent so much time by myself for years without being lonely.

Perhaps I had been lonely the entire time and only now realized it. Whatever the case, sitting in my apartment alone had lost its appeal today. It was an off day from the gym that I didn't want to ignore. Rest was just as important as rebuilding strength until I was back to top form, so going to the gym was out of the question. Going for a walk seemed aimless, unless...

I pulled out my phone and checked the housing listings within a few blocks, and was delighted to see there were nearly a dozen open houses. There would be more tomorrow as well. Not everything was within my budget, but looking couldn't hurt.

The first house I looked at was a mess. Not in the quaint, fixer-upper sense—it was a disaster. The duplex had been overhauled on the exterior fairly recently, yet the inside was nothing but trouble. A poor layout combined with the overwhelming probability of mold and loud neighbors screaming at each other eliminated this place from contemplation. It was a new listing with a price below market value, and after five minutes inside, it was clear why.

The second home was detached, which I preferred. Aside from having worn-down carpeting and needing fresh paint, there wasn't anything wrong with the two-bedroom home. It had a few modern updates in the kitchen and bathroom, but it didn't feel like the right fit.

Remy liked space, he always had. My apartment was small, but it was wide open aside from the bedroom. This house was much larger, but the rooms were all walled off and it felt... confining—even for me. Remy would hate being in a place like this, and I sure hoped he'd want to continue living with me.

Consulting him had crossed my mind. Buying a house was a huge commitment, and it was one I hoped he'd want to share with me. Remy lacked the means to contribute financially right now, but I still wanted to share it with him. I already knew he wouldn't be receptive to that without being able to help pay, so I kept it to myself.

Instead, I wanted to find a place we'd both love, then when he felt he was ready, we could add his name to the mortgage. Or something like that. The details weren't important to me; I just wanted my Rem. I felt like I almost had him too. A part of him sometimes seemed to doubt that we could make our relationship work again, and I imagine it had everything to do with why he'd left. Maybe in a few more weeks he'd be comfortable enough to tell me. I believed he'd told me most of his secrets, but that one was holding him back.

I'd waited ten years to have him back—I could wait a bit longer for this if it meant he'd be staying for good.

I DIDN'T USUALLY ENJOY BEING WOKEN up. That was until I opened my tired eyes and saw Remy's lips stretched around my cock, letting me know I was not dreaming. It took less than two minutes for me to spill down his throat and slump boneless against the mattress.

Remy sat up, smacked his lips and licked his fingers in a show that was way too seductive to be natural. "Happy birthday, Max. Thanks for breakfast." He paused, then tilted his head and crinkled his brow. "Although I suppose *I* should have got *you* breakfast in bed. Want some bacon, babe?"

I shot up and tackled him to the bed, pinning his hands next to his head. "I want you first."

He opened his mouth to speak, and I swallowed his reply in a kiss. Among other things.

Remy had insisted I go shower while he made me a "proper birthday breakfast." He used much more colorful language, though the cadence of his voice held excitement; he was definitely up to something. I showered, then followed the smell of bacon wafting down the hall from the kitchen. I found Remy writing something down on the back of an unopened letter next to my phone.

He glanced over at me, then went back to writing. "Hey. Your phone rang. I was going to leave it, but the call display said it was that Braddock guy. Hope it's okay I answered."

"Of course," I replied as I sat down beside him. "What did he say?"

Remy held up the letter and squinted to read his messy handwriting. "Um, he asked how you were doing, wished you a happy birthday, said you were missed, and he'd like you to come in tomorrow for a meeting at… ten. There's a little more here"—he handed me the letter and planted a quick kiss on my cheek—"but I have to go before that bacon catches on fire."

I looked over Remy's notes and frowned. Braddock wanted me to attend a briefing for managers. I hadn't given much thought to the promotion we'd briefly discussed before. In truth, I'd forgotten all about it. Braddock clearly had not.

"Don't even think about not going," Remy called out. "I already told him you'd be there."

I grunted low enough that Remy couldn't hear and tapped out an email to my boss confirming that I'd be at the meeting. He wrote me back immediately, asking if I could come twenty minutes earlier, which struck me as odd, but I said I would, then set my phone aside. I leaned back and started to drift back asleep when Remy hollered from the kitchen after a particularly loud pop. A string of hateful curses flew from his mouth, directed at the spattering bacon, and all I could do was grin.

Life with Remy used to be full of surprises and volatility.

We were young and still trying to figure out who we were and what we liked. We still were in many ways, but there was a definite shift. Now our lives could be described as mundane and domestic—and I couldn't think of anything I wanted more.

We spent the afternoon making out on the couch and watching TV—it was perfect. Remy checked his phone more often than he usually did, and I had a feeling it was regarding whatever he had planned. He hadn't mentioned us going anywhere, and we were hanging out in our underwear, so I wasn't expecting drop-ins.

Around seven in the evening, his knee began to bounce and his messages came in more frequently. He cursed under his breath while he replied to the latest one, and I couldn't take seeing him so stressed any longer.

"Rem, what's wrong?"

"Nothing."

"You're stressed."

"Am not."

"Your knee is bouncing."

He looked down at it, then planted his foot flat against the floor. "Fuck," he muttered.

I waited while he tapped out another message, growling at the reply this time. "Fine. I give up." He tossed his phone on the table and turned toward me with one knee pulled up. "Mac and I planned a surprise party for you. It's at his place, and I was supposed to lie to get you over there, but it's a shitty lie, and I don't want to worry you if I don't have to."

"Was it Macalister's idea?"

Remy rolled his eyes and nodded.

The corner of my mouth quirked up in a crooked grin. "What time are we supposed to be there?"

"At eight—but I'm not telling you anything else," he warned.

I held up my hands to signal my defeat. I'd let Remy and Macalister have their fun.

Remy knocked on the door to Macalister's place, which was eerily quiet. He answered the door—fully clothed, which was worth noting—with panicked eyes. Before he could get a word out, Remy held up a hand and shook his head.

"He already knows," Remy said flatly.

"Goddammit it, Remington Steele. You had one job," Macalister whined. He narrowed his eyes at Remy, then shifted his attention to me and pulled me into a backslapping hug. "Happy birthday, Maxim." He released me and pushed the door open all the way, revealing a room full of familiar faces and… strangely familiar, and rather gothic, decorations.

Everything clicked when I looked at the kitchen and saw a banner reading "Mystic Grill" hanging above the counter. All of my friends were dressed in a mix of dark casual clothes, leather jackets, Mystic Falls Timberwolves merch, and even a few burgundy cheerleader outfits. A smile spread across my lips when Macalister turned around and the name "Donovan" was printed on the back of his burgundy hoodie. I could so see him being Matt Donovan.

My throat tightened in the wake of all of the smiling faces directed at me, and I felt like I was about to do something stupid like cry when someone nudged my side. I turned to see Remy smiling up at me while the room broke out in a lively cheer, wishing me happy birthday. Before I could say anything, Macalister marched to the counter, grabbed his phone, then alt rock flooded the room. I instantly recognized it as the cover of "Enjoy the Silence" featured in season one.

"All right, dudes, back to the party," Macalister said, then winked at Remy.

Everyone's attention shifted from me to what looked like various games set up around the apartment. It was... perfect. Darts—which was brave, considering the amount of alcohol on the counter and red Solo cups in everyone's hands—Xbox, beer pong, *and* flip cup. It felt exactly like a high school or college party, down to everyone dressed as such.

"Do you like it?" Remy asked.

"This is too much. You guys didn't—"

"Nah-uh. That's not what I asked you."

"I love it," I answered quietly, my cheeks growing hot.

Remy pushed up on his toes and kissed my cheek as Macalister strode over and handed me a red cup of my own.

"I totally thought he was kidding when he said you liked *The Vampire Diaries*, man. Gotta say, this is pretty fun. You're going to flip when you see Dove and Taylor—they're around here somewhere. Taylor is some kind of witch, and Dove is sporting a long brown wig. I like him better blond, but it's kinda hot."

Taylor was one of Dubhlainn's friends, and a fellow drag queen. He must be Bonnie Bennett, and I'd guess Dubhlainn was Elena. I couldn't wait to see them. I caught a glimpse of blond hair in my periphery before Blake flung her arms around me and kissed my cheek.

"Happy birthday, Maxim," she said with a bright smile. I took in her cheerleader uniform, which suited her far too well, then tried and failed to fight back a smile. I'd never smiled so much in my life.

"Thank you, Ms. Forbes."

"Call me Caroline." She winked at me, then greeted Remy before continuing her rounds.

Remy squeezed my bicep and looked positively overjoyed. "There's another surprise." He stepped aside, revealing his younger sister.

"Rosalind," I said with a wide smile. She looked so much like Remy, and even had the same bleached hair he'd had when he'd arrived. His had grown out quite a bit, but hers was fresh.

"Hi, Maxy." Her tiny frame clung to me as she wrapped me up in a tight hug.

"Wait, why does she get away with calling you that but I can't?" Macalister whined beside me.

I shrugged and bit back a smile—rather unsuccessfully. "She's cuter than you."

Remy snickered on my other side while Macalister gaped at me, then at Rosalind. "You know, I should be at least mildly offended"—he turned his attention to Rosalind —"but you are pretty freaking cute. Hi, I'm Mac." He extended his hand, but Remy intercepted it.

"Nope. Hands to yourself, Ken Doll."

"Um, are you her keeper?"

"No, I'm her brother," Remy said, squeezing Macalister's hand harder.

I rolled my eyes and sighed to cover a snicker. They looked like a couple of bickering cartoon characters, tugging their joined hands back and forth in a show of manliness. As entertaining as it was, I knew I should break it up soon.

Dubhlainn appeared at Macalister's side and elbowed him in the ribs, causing Macalister to release Remy's hand. "Is my fella botherin' ya, miss?"

Rosalind arched a brow at Dubhlainn then shook her head. "Not at all. He and my brother were just having a dick measuring contest, though I don't recall seeing that on tonight's itinerary."

Dubhlainn whistled while Remy and Macalister stood speechless. "I see. Behave, gentlemen. Happy birthday,

Maxim." Dubhlainn gave me a friendly nod then dragged Macalister off toward the beer pong table.

Remy, Rosalind, and I sat on the high stools at the counter while we caught up on each other's lives. Remy had been a decent middleman, but hearing how successful Rosalind was doing from her own lips made me eternally proud. Seeing that she also hadn't caved to her parents' wishes and maintained her alternative lifestyle and look deepened that pride for the woman she'd become.

Bryan was in the kitchen making hors d'oeuvres, sporting brown, pointy ears, a tail, and a painted nose and drawn whiskers. He looked adorably cute and not at all like a werewolf. I'd snickered when I first saw him after Remy whispered "Big Bad Wolf" to me.

Eli kept himself busy by ferrying out fresh food and hanging out in the kitchen unless Axel or Santi dragged him out for a round of flip cup. He wasn't any good at it, but they were determined to teach him.

Throughout the night, people came by individually or in small groups to give me birthday wishes and check in on my recovery. I knew I'd have to thank Remy and Macalister for keeping everyone entertained. I'd managed to stay out of the spotlight and hadn't once felt overwhelmed.

And then Macalister poured shots.

The night became fuzzy after the seventh.

The ride home was quiet, though it was far from uncomfortable. I held Remy's hand and drifted off in the back of the Uber. He woke me when we got back to the apartment. I only vaguely remember Remy dragging me inside, undressing me, and getting me into bed.

I must have dosed off again because when I opened my

eyes next, Remy was standing next to the bed holding a glass of water, which he handed me. "Drink up, big guy. You'll thank me in the morning."

I did as he asked, then passed the glass back. He set it on the nightstand, then sat on the edge of the bed.

"I can't thank you enough, Rem. Not just for tonight, but for everything." I teased a sliver of exposed skin on his lower back, then let my hand fall. "I can't believe you and Macalister worked together."

Remy rolled his eyes then pulled his shirt over his head. "You could try to look a little less pleased about it. You have no idea how much I suffered being around that guy so much."

"He's not so bad. You're just being grumpy."

He got under the covers with a sigh and propped himself up on an elbow, facing me. "Compared to how stressed I was looking around here for a candle on Valentine's Day, dealing with Mac was relatively easy. I thought I was going to pull all my fucking hair out from stress last month. I tore through all the closets, then had to fix everything in very little time."

My smile morphed into wide-eyed panic and my gaze flicked to the bedroom closet before going back to Remy. Had he found our old rings?

"What's wrong?" he asked with furrowed brows.

"Did you go through my closet?"

"No. I looked in the hall closets. I swear I didn't rifle through your things. Well, I kinda did, but not in here. I'm sor—"

"No. Don't apologize, love. You didn't do anything wrong at all." I scrubbed my hands over my face and let out a heavy sigh in an effort to relax. "I'm sorry for acting strangely. I'm just tired." I lifted my arm and Remy snuggled in close, lightly tracing his fingertips over the scars on my shoulder.

"You're not mad?"

"I promise I'm not. Anything but, actually. Tonight was a lot of fun."

"Thank fuck."

I huffed a laugh then rubbed up and down his back. "It makes me really happy to know you're getting along with Macalister now."

Remy scoffed, though it was exaggerated. "Easy, big guy. He and I won't be going on play dates or some shit."

I hummed in amusement and it turned into a yawn. It had been a beautiful day, but a tiring one. I closed my eyes and was half asleep when I felt warm fingers creep under the band of my trunks and cup my balls. I moaned low and deep, half from pleasure and half from fatigue.

"Don't mind me. You can sleep if you want. I'm sure I can entertain myself." Remy squeezed my already hardening cock despite his words. I opened an eye to see him grinning wolfishly.

"I thought you were going to entertain yourself."

"Oh, I am. I'm going to use your big dick, but I'll be doing all the work."

A cross between a huff and a moan fell from my lips as Remy's thumb circled my tip. "I'm feeling rather involved right now."

"One, it's your birthday, and there's no way in hell you're not gonna get some. Two, I'm horny as fuck right now, and I wanna ride you until one of us passes out." He pulled my trunks off, then rolled into my lap, already free of his sleep pants. "I'll be honest, if you do pass out on me and you're still hard, I'm gonna keep going, babe."

My eyes shot open and I grabbed his wrists, stilling his exploratory hands. "Remy."

"Yes, Maxim?" he asked, voice dripping with lust.

I thought he might be riling me up again—trying to get me to be rough with him—but when I heard his voice and looked in his eyes, I saw that he wasn't after that. There was a vulnerable need radiating off of him that I couldn't deny. I released his wrists and laced my fingers behind my head; I'd let him take whatever he wanted from me.

I didn't have to speak. The action and his resulting wide smile told me he understood perfectly clear. He somehow always did.

He leaned across me and reached for the nightstand drawer, which added more pressure against our bare cocks. I bit the inside of my cheek and managed not to moan. If Remy was in a mood, he might tease me all night just to see how much noise he could draw from me. It wouldn't have been the first time.

His lips found mine at the same time I heard him pump lube into his hand. His tongue distracted me from thinking about where that hand was going, though it became clear when he sucked in a short breath and lost his rhythm kissing me.

I cupped his face and took control while he worked at getting himself ready for me. We hadn't had sex this way since I stopped wearing my brace, and even then, Remy hadn't seemed as desperate for it. His movements weren't frantic and jerky, but his entire body radiated with need for me. I saw it in his eyes, felt it in his touch, heard it in his voice, and I could taste it on his tongue.

His slicked hand suddenly closed around my cock, stroking me from base to tip and coating me in slippery lubricant. I'd been hasty in prepping him before, but this was way too fast. Trying to voice that while Remy's hand worked my cock and his mouth was latched on to my neck was impossible. He knew what he was doing, and he knew it was going to hurt.

Remy placed one last kiss on my parted lips before he sat up and lined himself up with my painfully hard cock. His steely blue gaze locked on me, then he slowly lowered himself, not stopping or slowing as I breached him. His eyes went wide, then his brows furrowed as garbled cries fell from his mouth. He felt hot and tight around me, and I was scared to move—to even breathe until he adjusted.

"Fucking hell, babe," he hissed through clenched teeth. He rose up a fraction of an inch and dragged his blunt nails down my chest, leaving a sting in their wake that only served to heighten my arousal.

My cock twitched at the added stimulation, and Remy's eyes fluttered. He took a deep breath, then rose up a few inches on his thighs before sinking back down on an exhale. I slammed my eyes closed and my skin prickled from the sensation and the sounds of his ragged cries. He worked up a steady rhythm, and I rubbed his thighs, occasionally squeezing his ass hard enough to leave marks.

Remy bit his lip and nodded down at me before he flicked one of my nipples—hard. Before I could think about what I was doing, I slapped his ass. A stinging heat spread from my palm to the tips of my fingers while Remy winced and moved faster.

He liked it.

I slapped the other cheek and he cried out, losing his timing for a few beats. Another slap to the first cheek had him leaning all the way forward, kissing and nipping at my mouth like he couldn't get enough. Remy panted my name repeatedly, followed by one word: more.

I grabbed the globes of his ass and held him in place while I drove my hips up, sliding my cock in him as far as I could. He wrapped his arms around my neck and under my shoulder and clung to me with everything he had as our bodies moved together. I let a hand slide off of his ass and up his back, in favor of cupping his nape. Remy's sharp intake of breath on every stroke was loud in my ear and told me I was hitting his prostate. He wouldn't last much longer with this new angle, and neither would I.

His breaths came out faster and shallower, and his hold on me tightened. He squeezed me so tightly that it was almost painful, then his body tensed and went slack as he shot ribbons of cum between us. I fucked him through it and unloaded in him not even six thrusts later.

We lay unmoving, aside from our heaving chests. My spent cock slipped free of him, and I felt my cum follow, dripping down my groin. Not caring enough to move and get cleaned up, I kissed Remy's sweat-dampened hair and held him.

We fell asleep just like that, a sweaty, sticky mess, and I wouldn't have had it any other way.

SIXTEEN

REMY

As DESPERATE AS I WAS for a shower, I hadn't had the energy to get up early and shower with Maxim before he left to go meet with his boss. I lay in bed with dried cum on my stomach and taint. Fucking glamorous. The sheets were just as messy as I was, but everything could wait a few more hours.

I'd nearly fallen back asleep when my phone rang on the nightstand. Apparently I'd been too preoccupied with getting Maxim to bed, then getting in his pants to set it to vibrate. An irritated groan forced its way out of me, and I rolled away from the phone, ducking under the covers.

No one calls me except Maxim. The thought had me turning over and reaching for the phone too fast, and I knocked it onto the floor. I hung over the side of the bed and felt around for it in the dark, but it'd stopped ringing by the time I found it.

Call history showed an LA number that I didn't recognize, and I wondered if it had been one of my old friends trying to reconnect. But them calling would be... odd. Especially this early. My phone said it was just after eight, and it was two hours earlier in Cali—no one I knew would be awake at six a.m. by choice. No one except—

A notification for a voicemail popped up on my screen. I took a deep breath and tapped on it, then turned it on speaker. I said a silent prayer that the voice on the message wouldn't be Stan's, but fate was a cruel bitch.

"Check your emails, Remington," was all he'd said. Four words were enough to make my spine prickle and my gut twist. Wondering what the fuck he wanted, I opened up my emails and cursed under my breath when I saw a new one from him.

I wanted to delete it again—I really did. The prospect of receiving another call from him if I didn't read this and respond seemed so much worse, though. With trembling hands, I opened the message and dread immediately seeped into every fiber of my being. He wanted money—repayment for my flight, my phone bill, my weekly allowance when I'd left, my fucking scripts…

I should have seen this coming. Stan had a total of nearly ten thousand dollars at the bottom of the message. PrEP alone was almost two-grand a month because I didn't have health insurance, and he'd gotten it for me in three-month increments. He was even threatening legal action against me for stealing his credit card if I didn't repay him within three days.

I was fucked. Completely and utterly fucked, and I had no one to blame but myself.

My mind raced through all of the ways I could get that sum of money together quickly. It wasn't anything to a family like mine, but the odds of my parents giving it to me without asking questions were pretty fucking nonexistent. My MacBook was worth a couple grand, but unless I seriously underpriced it, it would take too long to sell.

Asking Maxim wasn't an option. He'd give me the money

with no questions asked, and I couldn't do that to him. I'd left in the first place because I was terrible for him, and I should have left again after he could take care of himself. I was a fucking idiot for letting myself believe that I was anything more than what I was: tainted. There was something seriously wrong with me, and I'd ruin Maxim if I stayed. He'd never choose to leave me, so I had to do it.

I'd known this since I'd first fucked up ten years ago, and as much as I tried to convince myself things could be different, they weren't. I hadn't changed, and that was the problem. Maxim deserved better than a cheating, lying whore. He knew about the lying, but I hadn't found the stones to tell him that I was a fucking cheater too. It would break his heart, more than me abruptly leaving had.

I pushed the blankets back and climbed out of bed. If I only had a few days to come up with the money, I couldn't afford to wallow in bed. I'd start with my bank—that's what people did when they needed money. I could get a loan, then worry about getting a job to make payments.

I gathered up the soiled bedding out of habit and threw it in the washer. I'd turn it on after I had a shower, then head straight for my bank, and hope everything would work out okay.

"I'm sorry, Mr. Kincaid" were the last words I heard before I drowned out the financial advisor sitting across from me. It hadn't occurred to me that unemployed assholes with bad credit couldn't just waltz into a bank and get loans. I left the bank feeling ten times worse about my situation, if that were even possible.

The reality of my situation was setting in, and it made my throat dry. Pride be damned, I had to go see my parents. I'd get on my knees and beg if I had to.

My fist fell heavily on the door. I'd already rung the bell several times and was getting antsy. What if no one was home? They could have easily been on vacation or out for tea, or whatever the fuck pretentious rich people did at—I checked my phone—nearly eleven on a Thursday morning.

The distant click of heels grew louder from inside the house, then my mother appeared behind the cracked door. Her eyes widened for a second when she saw me before she schooled her expression.

"Remington, you've come back."

"Yeah, I-ah was hoping to talk to you and Dad about something." I put my hands in my pockets to keep from fidgeting. She'd always hated that.

"Your father is away on business."

"Well, can I talk to you then?" My voice sounded desperate, even to my own ears.

Her cold gaze raked me over disapprovingly and she held her ground. "I don't think that's wise, Remington."

I swallowed the lump in my throat and nodded. "Fine. That's fine. I just need some money from my trust or something. Just ten grand—I'll even pay it back."

"Get yourself cleaned up. Don't come back until then." Her words punched me in the gut, then she closed and locked the door in my face.

Getting the money from her was a longshot, but I hadn't foreseen being denied entry to the house and being turned away like a fucking unwanted salesman. Too ashamed to knock again, I turned and headed down the long driveway, trying to think of another plan.

Just fucking tell Maxim, a small part of me urged—the part that wanted to be selfish and stay. He would pay, and then we could go on being happy. So what if I never had to take any responsibility for my actions? It would be status quo. I was good at taking—no, I was great at it. My parasitic self thrived on others, but I couldn't do it to Maxim.

Walking always gave me too much fucking time to think, and as such, my mind wandered. Given my history with drugs, I probably looked like a desperate junkie to my mother. I wasn't into anything too serious when I was younger—okay, coke was serious depending on whom you asked—but they'd threatened to cut me off over it. They didn't actually do it until I refused to leave Maxim.

Maxim never liked when I used drugs either. He'd asked me to stop, and I did. I fucking did for months. I wasn't an addict, I just liked how they made me feel and my friends were into it. It sounds so stupid and juvenile to think about it in those terms, but that's exactly what it was. I'd relapsed the day after Maxim had proposed to me. I was the happiest I'd ever been, and I went to see my friends while Maxim was in class. Everyone gave me their congratulations, and I'd had a lot to drink. By the time I got to Jonas Welliver's apartment, I was fucking blitzed.

He'd been one of my oldest friends—we grew up together doing the same rich kid bullshit, and we'd rebelled together over the years. When I told him about Maxim and me, he'd suggested we celebrate with a few bumps. I refused at first, but he'd insisted, and I was too damn drunk to remain steadfast.

A few bumps turned into enough lines to spell my full name, and I lost control. I ended up letting Jonas fuck me while I snorted every last bit of coke he slid my way. When I'd woken up, I had several missed calls from Maxim, as well as a few from Mac and my sister.

I'd panicked and gone back to our apartment, but he'd already gone to class for the day. He left me a note, and reading it was what broke me. "I hope you're okay. Please call me when you come home, love." I felt like the biggest piece of shit then, and I didn't know how I could possibly look him in the eye after what I'd done. Being drunk and high was no excuse; I shouldn't have been there in the first place. Jonas and I had drifted apart after I got together with Maxim. Max got a bad feeling from him, and I'd respected that. I was just too fucking happy after he proposed, and I'd wanted to tell the whole world. I was stupid, and I should have known better.

Instead of making excuses and destroying Maxim, I chose to leave. I knew it would hurt him, but he'd recover from it. If I stayed, he'd forgive me, and I'd inevitably hurt him again. I couldn't do that to him, so I packed up my shit and left like a coward before he got home. I left my ring on his note along with a few words of my own: "I'm so sorry."

An icy gust of wind chilled me, jarring me from thoughts of the past. I tried not to think about that day and what it must have been like when Maxim got home. But he'd turned out okay; I'd seen it with my own eyes these past few months. He would be okay again without me.

I made it to the gas station and locked myself inside the washroom while I figured out what to do. All of my old friends in the city had moved on. I broke ties with everyone when I left, and calling up out of the blue would no doubt get me a few "fuck yous" and laughter. Those people would rather watch me burn. There was one person I could try, though. Someone who wouldn't care about the time or distance between us. I took a deep breath to calm my nerves as I tapped out a text to my sister, asking her if she still had Jonas's number.

"IMAGINE my surprise when I saw your fuckin' name on my

call display." Jonas raked a hand through his freshly cut blond hair and grinned at me like I was his prey. "How long has it been?"

"Around ten years." I ignored that fact that he kept my number in his contacts after so long. It wasn't important.

"Wild, man." He sat back in his chair adjacent to me and spread his legs wide in a casual stance. "So what can I do for you? I'm assuming you called for a reason."

"I need to borrow some money."

He hummed, though it sounded more amused than contemplative. "And why would I do that?"

"Call it a favor for old time's sake. It's only ten thousand, and I really need it, Jonas." I cringed at the desperation that had crept into my voice.

"Jonas—not even Joey anymore." He hummed again, then drummed his fingers on the tops of his thighs. "You might not remember, but I'm not the charitable type, Remy. And not to be rude, but I don't have a lot of faith in your ability to repay me. Am I wrong?"

My knee started bouncing, though I made myself stop when Jonas's gaze flicked down to my nervous tick. "I'll figure something out."

"I can see that you're desperate, though my answer is still no. But," he added abruptly, cutting me off before I could beg, "I might know a way you can earn it."

The playful lilt of his voice unnerved me. Jonas was trouble when we were kids—I had no idea what he could possibly be involved in now. Fucking rich kids.

"I'll do anything."

"That's the perfect attitude for what I had in mind. Let me reach out to some friends and see if they're still seeking entertainment for a private party tomorrow. You're older than they typically like, but the tattoos will be appealing. Do you follow?"

I didn't need a degree to read between the lines. My gut twisted, and I clenched my teeth to keep my expression neutral. "I understand. I'll do whatever I have to do to get the money."

"Sick. We'll discuss rates once I've heard back from them. Do you know your status?"

I nodded. "Negative on all fronts."

"Hard limits? That will decrease the price."

"None."

"You're giving me all the right answers, Remy. Care to tell me why you need the money so badly? I can't imagine that your family has gone broke and can't bail you out for what is essentially pocket change."

"If it's all the same to you, I'd rather not talk about it. It doesn't change anything."

He arched his brows at me, then studied me from head to toe, long enough to make me uncomfortable. "Fair enough. Make yourself comfortable. I'm going to make a few calls."

I swallowed a sharp laugh. Comfortable—*Fucking hilarious.*

By the time I left Jonas's condo, I felt hollow. We'd gone over what would be expected of me, and every word he said plunged me deeper into resignation. It wasn't anything I hadn't done before, and I'd come out of this. He'd even been "kind enough," as he'd put it, to give me poppers.

On the ride home I contemplated finishing what I'd started that evening in Palm Springs when the hospital called. I'd lost all will to live up until then, but things had changed. I didn't know when it'd happened, but being with Maxim again had killed my resolve to go through with dying. I'd been so sure that it was the only choice, and now at my lowest point, I couldn't even bring myself to do it. Perhaps I was meant to live on and fucking suffer a bit longer—lord knows I deserved it. I couldn't say those feelings wouldn't come back after another few years without him. They probably would. I'd deal with it then.

Maxim was home when I got back. I stuck to a partial truth and said I'd gone to see my mother again when he asked where I'd been. It turned out to be the perfect explanation for my shitty mood, and he didn't press. If he had, I feared I would have spilled everything.

We had a quiet evening, and the next morning was very much the same. I walked with Maxim to the gym in the afternoon, then went back to the apartment to gather up my shit. I couldn't take it with me in case the guys I was meeting up with were the type to steal from me. I wouldn't exactly be in a position to stop it. And at least I could say a proper goodbye to Maxim this way.

I'd at least give him that courtesy this time.

SEVENTEEN

MAXIM

I couldn't shake the feeling that something was wrong with Remy. He'd told me he went to see his mom, but his mood still seemed off. He was distant and was trying to hide it. His efforts made it obvious that he didn't want to talk about it, so I'd let it go for the night. He really was the worst liar.

Then he'd been acting strange this morning too. I hadn't wanted to leave, though I didn't want to suffocate him either. His behavior had been so strange that I'd forgotten to tell him about my meeting with Braddock, and he hadn't even asked. That should have been my first clue that something wasn't right with him; he would have normally asked me about it as soon as he saw me. Especially since it was regarding a possible promotion.

"Are you all right, man? You seem a bit"—Macalister waved his hand in front of him—"distracted or something."

I sighed noncommittally then rolled my eyes and decided to be frank with him. "I'm worried about Remy."

"Why?"

"He was acting strange last night and this morning. It's

probably nothing, but I can't shake the feeling that something is wrong."

Macalister's forehead creased. "Wanna wrap up early today? You're obviously not going to stop thinking about Remington Steele, so you might as well go home and talk to him."

I nodded and set my weights back on the rack. "Thank you. I'm sorry."

"Nah, it's cool. Dove is home today anyway. You want a ride back?"

"That's okay. Walking will give me some time to think."

Macalister held out his fist, and I bumped it with mine. "All right, dude. Text me later."

I arrived home twenty minutes later to a quiet apartment, and that uneasy feeling in my stomach began to swell. "Rem," I called out as I toed out of my boots and hung up my jacket. No answer came and I went straight for the bedroom, hoping he was merely asleep. Remy wasn't there. His bag, however, was fully packed and resting against the wall near the door.

He couldn't be leaving. *Not again.* His stuff, although packed, was still here, which had to mean he was coming back. I was about to call him when I noticed a piece of paper on the nightstand. I strode over, picked it up, and felt my heart sink.

I can't do this. I'm so sorry about everything.
I'll be back later to get my stuff.

"No, no, no, please, no." I dropped the note and called Remy. I paced around the room like a caged animal, my nerves fraying more with each ring that went unanswered.

His voicemail kicked in and I left him a message to please call me back before I hung up and dialed him again.

No answer again. I checked my texts and didn't see any from him. I sent him one, again asking for him to call, then I called Rosalind.

"Hello?" she answered in a tired voice.

"It's Maxim. I'm sorry if I woke you, but have you heard from Remy today?"

"No, sorry. Is he okay?" the tired edge in her voice switched to concern.

"I don't know. I can't reach him. He left a note saying he'd be back later, but something feels wrong."

"I'll call around and see if I can find him." She took a breath as if she was going to say something, then cut herself off. "He might be involved in some shit, Max. He called me yesterday for the number of one of his old friends. The guy was a douche back then, and he's grown into an even bigger asshole."

"Who is it?"

"Jonas Welliver. You used to know him too."

The name sounded so familiar. I couldn't quite place him, though. *Think, think.* "Do you mean Joey?"

"Yeah, that's the one."

I felt like I was going to be sick. I'd hated him back then and thought he was dangerous. Remy hadn't seen it, but Joey was a predator and a user; why would Remy want to talk to him now?

"Thank you. Please call me if you hear anything."

"You do the same."

I hung up, then called Macalister on my way out to the living room. He answered on the second ring.

"What's up, Maxy?"

"Remy's gone," I choked out. I didn't mean to sound so dramatic, but I didn't have the strength to hide my feelings.

"What do you mean?" His tone changed from his usual playfulness to serious.

"He left a note saying he was sorry and that he'd be back for his things, and he won't answer his phone. Rosalind hasn't heard from him either."

"Breathe, Max. I'll help you track him down. I can be there in twenty." I heard rustling around and Dubhlainn in the background asking what was wrong.

"I'm sorry to bother you—"

"It's no bother. I'm leaving right now." Dubhlainn's muffled voice became audible again, and he and Macalister had a quick exchange. "Hey, do you and Remy use the Find My Friends app? Dove said you can track the location of his phone that way."

I shook my head before I realized he couldn't see me. "No. I have no idea what that is."

"Does he have a MacBook?"

"Yes."

"You can see his iMessages on that. You might be able to find out where he went."

I ran back to my room and hesitated a moment before going through Remy's bag. I hated violating his privacy, but I had to find him. I pulled his laptop out, then sat down right there on the floor.

"It's password protected," I groaned.

"Try it until I get there. I should be able to get access in a few minutes. I've gotta go now. I'm just getting in the car."

"Thank you."

"It'll be okay, Max. We'll find him."

I swallowed the lump in my throat and disconnected the call. I tried variations of Remy's birthday, then his old password from when we were younger. Both were incorrect, and I was too worked up to think. What if I couldn't find him and he didn't come back? What if he did come back, only to leave again? I couldn't let that happen. Something had him spooked. Maybe if I could get it out of him, he might stay. I had no idea what it could possibly be, and I felt powerless.

I hadn't felt this powerless since the first time Remy had left, and before that, since before I'd met him. My mind drifted back to his note—I couldn't make sense of it. He'd seemed happier since January and had stopped talking about leaving. He wasn't without his problems, but he was making strides toward getting better—or at least I thought he was. Had I been too blinded by my own selfish desires and missed that Remy was still struggling? I didn't think that was the case, but clearly something was wrong.

I stared at the blank password field on the screen and sighed. He kept secrets from me, but I still knew him better than anyone else, even with the years apart. I took a few deep breaths and tried to calm myself down enough to think. Remy, aside from his troubles, was not a complicated man. He wouldn't have an elaborate, random password or anything that wasn't important to him.

Trying "password" felt insulting, but I tried it anyway and was met with another incorrect response. I drummed my fingers lightly across the keys, then typed in my birthday. On the third try with only numbers, I gained access and breathed a sigh of relief.

I said a silent apology for the egregious invasion of privacy I was about to commit, then opened up Remy's messages. Right at the top was a number not assigned to a contact. I clicked on it, then scrolled through the few exchanged messages. There was an address listed over in Wicker Park that I jotted down, along with a message confirming payment.

Remy's messages were limited to one-word replies, though the latest message from today was left unanswered.

Perk up, man. You might even enjoy this if you relax.

Those words sent a chill down my spine. What had he gotten himself into now? And why hadn't he told me? I could have sat and wracked my brain all day while I waited for him, but the pull to go get him was too strong. Whatever this was sounded unsavory and I felt compelled to bring Remy home as soon as possible.

I got up and headed for the front door where I slipped back into my boots and jacket. I sincerely hoped I was misreading this situation, and that Remy would be angry when I arrived—but he'd be safe. I went outside to wait for Macalister, not wanting to waste a second more than necessary. Remy had to be okay. I didn't know what I'd do if he wasn't.

THE DULL THUMP of heavy bass and muffled raucous voices floated through the door of the condo Remy was supposedly in. I'd gotten lucky and was let in by a young woman leaving with her dog. The timing was perfect, considering I was a few more seconds away from losing the composure I was known for and breaking the glass door.

Mac had offered to come up with me, though I'd asked him to stay in the car. If there was some sort of trouble inside, I didn't want to drag him into it. I pounded on the door with enough force to rattle the hinges. There was no way someone inside wouldn't be able to hear it over the music.

The music continued and I was about to knock louder when a man around my age with dampened hair answered the door. His dress shirt was open and his pants were undone and sat lopsided on his hips. A closer look at him, and I could see that he was sweating and his chest was heaving.

"Yeah—what?"

"Sorry to intrude. I'm looking for someone and—"

"This is a private party." He started to close the door, but I blocked it with my foot.

"Have you seen this man?" I held up my phone with a picture of Remy open.

"I think you're in the wrong place, guy." He tried to close the door again, his forehead creasing in frustration when I didn't move.

"I have reason to believe he's here."

"Never seen the guy before. You need to…"

The guy kept talking, but a loud smack followed by laughter had my attention shifting over his shoulder. The guy in front of me wasn't big, yet I couldn't see much because of the angle. I saw the bare shoulders of one—no, two—men, and heard at least four distinct voices.

He tried to shove me back at the same time another crack reached my ears, followed by the pained cry of the man I loved more than anything in this world. I moved in a daze fueled by rage and the need to get to him. The gatekeeping guy's wrist and nose suffered as a result of that as I twisted his arm and forced the door open, sending it slamming into his face.

There were five men in various states of undress standing in the cleared-out living room. They surrounded another man who knelt on the floor and had someone's hand fisted in his hair, and another's cock shoved down his throat. I couldn't see his face, but the unmistakable black-and-purple floral tattoo on his back confirmed what I'd feared.

It took a few seconds for them to realize I'd barged in, then three of the men turned to me—or rather their friend on the floor behind me.

"Who the fuck are you?" one of them yelled.

I ignored him and advanced toward Remy, whose head was still being forced onto the man in front of him. Each step raised a murderous intent within me so powerful that I didn't trust myself not to do something terrible to these men. Violence was never my goal, and I never tried to use my size for intimidation, but I'd engage in both if I had to.

"Get your fucking hands off of him," I spat out with enough venom to make the guy holding Remy's head take a step back. Then another.

Remy went stock-still on the floor for a moment then whipped his head around. His pupils were blown, swallowing most of the cold blue of his irises, and his cheek was red where he'd been slapped.

"Hey, what the fuck do you think you're doing, asshole?" the guy in front of Remy said.

I ignored him and grabbed Remy's arm, pulling him to his feet. He was missing his shirt, though his pants were still on. Thank God. I looked him over quickly, and he seemed unharmed aside from his reddening cheek. He wouldn't meet my gaze, but I'd worry about that once we were out of this place.

I turned us toward the door and started walking, only to be stopped by the initial gatekeeper and another two men.

"Leave the bitch and get the fuck out. We paid for the entire night."

Remy flinched and looked away, remaining silent.

"Get out of the way," I said through clenched teeth. This wasn't a movie. None of these men seemed to be in top shape, let alone trained fighters. I didn't have any training either, but I was confident in my ability to get through them if I had to.

"Gentlemen," a familiar voice called from the doorway. Macalister stepped inside the condo pointedly twirling his baseball bat in his hands. "You're making quite the fucking ruckus in here. Do I need to call the cops?"

Not wanting that kind of drama, the men stepped aside and let Remy and me pass. One of them shouted something about wanting their money back as we left the unit, Macalister right behind us. Once the elevator doors closed behind us, Macalister let the bat fall to his side and we both released a deep sigh. Remy remained silent.

Macalister looked at me questioningly, and I shook my head. I owed him my gratitude, though now wasn't the time for it. I had to take care of Remy, and Macalister seemed to understand that. I took off my jacket and draped it over Remy's bare shoulders then tipped his chin up so I could look him in the eye.

"It's okay, love."

His bottom lip trembled, then he sucked in a sharp breath and the tears started. I held him close during the drive home. A twenty-minute drive turned into thirty with traffic yet Macalister maintained his calm and didn't add to the tension in the car. Remy sat in my lap in the backseat and cried and trembled in my arms the whole ride home. I didn't know what to say, so I held him and gently rubbed his back while my heart bled for him.

He'd stopped crying by the time we got dropped off at home, though he still wouldn't willingly raise his gaze to mine or speak. I led him inside, then to the bathroom after a short deliberation. I wanted to get him into bed, but I had a feeling he'd want today washed away first. In more than just the literal sense.

I turned the water on, then carefully undressed him when he made no attempt to do it himself, mindful that he could have bruises I couldn't yet see.

"Come on, Rem," I cooed, trying to get him under the shower spray. I'd never seen him so defeated. He was acting

like a zombie—completely devoid of life. Without his coop-
eration, I succeeded in getting water all over the floor and my
clothes. Now that I fully understood how difficult it was to
help someone shower while you were fully dressed, I stripped
down to my trunks and got in with him.

I started with shampooing his hair, massaging his scalp
how he liked, then lathered up my hands and gliding them
over every inch of him. I kept my touch as light and unob-
trusive as possible while still being effective at the task at
hand. Remy still hadn't spoken, and he swayed a bit, looking
utterly exhausted.

I skipped conditioner in favor of getting him off of his
feet before he collapsed. After shutting the water off, I
wrapped him in a large towel, then sat him down on the
closed toilet lid. Droplets of water fell from his lashes in place
of the tears he'd already shed before I dabbed them dry. I
couldn't see him cry any more today.

"Do you want your toothbrush, love?"

His eyes flicked to mine for a moment, then he nodded
with the slightest of movements. While he brushed his teeth,
I dried myself off and wrapped a towel around my waist after
taking off my wet underwear.

A small spark of relief hit me when Remy moved to rinse
out the toothpaste. It wasn't much, but it was more than I'd
seen from him in the last hour. He returned his toothbrush
to the cup on the sink and turned toward me. His eyes were
bloodshot and the dilation in his pupils had reduced. Whatever he'd been on was likely short-lasting.

"Do you want to lie down?" I asked, rubbing his fore-
arms with the pads of my thumbs.

His head tipped down in a small nod, and I led him to
the bedroom. He got in without any fuss and curled up on
his side facing me. I got in beside him, mirroring his stance.
The curtains were closed so it took a few minutes for my

eyes to adjust to the darkness before I could clearly see him again.

I thought he might have fallen asleep, but his eyes were still open and he was watching me, worrying his bottom lip. I felt like I should say something, yet no words came. Where did I even start? I wanted to tell him everything would be okay, but I knew Remy, and he wouldn't believe me if I made a blind promise like that. I had to hear the whole story first, and I had to wait for him to tell it.

Minutes turned into an hour while the silence stretched on between us. My phone went off a few times in the bathroom where I'd left it, and I realized I'd forgotten to text Rosalind back. I'd apologize to her later—I wasn't moving from Remy's side.

"Why," Remy started in a low, hoarse voice. "Why are you still being so kind to me?"

"I love you."

He sucked in a breath and sniffled.

"I love you," I repeated. "I still do."

"I cheated on you. Back then. I'm not a good person." His voice cracked on the same word that made me feel like I was going to be sick. "It was the day after you proposed. I was so fucking happy, Max. I felt like I was getting everything I'd ever wanted, and I wanted to tell everyone I knew. I got drunk and high and fucked someone else that night."

The words hurt—they really did—but the sorrow radiating from Remy hurt even more. Not wanting to trivialize his admission, I considered how to best reply to him before I answered. "Tell me about it."

"What?"

"What else happened? You weren't doing drugs anymore at that point, so why that night?"

"Um, I was drunk. From visiting a few other people. I wasn't thinking clearly when I got to Jonas's place."

Jonas. I managed to swallow my anger, though my face must have had a tell because Remy stopped talking.

"I'm really sorry. You'd warned me about him, and I didn't listen." Fresh tears welled in Remy's eyes, and I wiped them away. "He offered me some coke. I turned him down a few times, but I eventually caved. A little turned into a lot and the next thing I knew he was fucking me in his bed. I'm not trying to make excuses or ask for forgiveness. I know what I did was horrible and inexcusable. I—" An involuntary shudder cut him off, and he sniffled again. "I didn't know what to say to you. I'd fucked everything up so badly, and I've done it again."

He broke into a sob, and I couldn't hold back any longer. I pulled him into my arms and held him as his body trembled and his tears dampened my skin. I waited until he calmed down before I spoke again.

"That's why you left, then."

I felt him nod. "I knew I'd done something unforgivable and—"

"No, Rem. I *would* have forgiven you."

"I know you would have." Remy pulled away, then sat up with the blanket pulled up to his neck. I sat up too, wondering where he was going with this. "You would have forgiven me, and I would have promised that it wouldn't happen again. You would have carried that hurt around, and I didn't want to make you feel like that. I left because I knew something like it would happen again, and you'd forgive me. I could see it so clearly, Max. I'd continue to hurt you, and I wouldn't let that happen."

"You can't know that for sure."

"Can't I? Look at us now. I fucked up again, and you're not mad."

I shook my head once. "I'm furious, Rem. But I'm also hurt, not just for me, but for you."

"That's why I left! I didn't want you feeling that way, especially not about me once you knew the truth."

A sad smile spread across my lips, and I took his hand. "Not knowing was so much worse. I spent years wondering what I'd done wrong. You left me with no closure, and I'd assumed the worst—that maybe you didn't love me as much as I thought and I'd scared you away when I proposed."

"Oh, fucking hell." He buried his face in his hands, then smoothed them through his wild hair, tugging at the back. "That was never my intention. I swear it never even crossed my mind. See? I fuck everything up."

"What happened today?" I asked, hoping the change in topic would stop Remy from hyperventilating.

"I got an email from Stan a few weeks ago. I deleted it without opening it. Two days ago, he left me a voicemail telling me to check my email. There was a new one from him. It basically outlined everything I owed him and threatened legal action if I didn't pay him back by tomorrow. I tried the bank and my parents first—I didn't lie about going to see my mom again. She wouldn't even let me inside the fucking house." He laughed bitterly and scratched at the raven on his neck. "I thought of Jonas while I was walking back down the driveway. Of all of my old friends, he was the only person I could think of who wouldn't hate me for cutting ties so suddenly. I got his number from Roz. He was so smug when he saw me. He didn't give me the cash, but he said I could earn it, and that he knew some guys... you know the rest."

"Why didn't you just tell me?" I was frustrated—perhaps more than I'd ever been—though I kept my voice even.

"Because it wasn't your fucking problem. If I'd told you, you'd have paid Stan, and I'd have been right all along."

"Right about what?"

"That I'd continue to hurt and use you if I stayed."

I took hold of one of his hands and brushed my thumbs along his inner wrist. I waited to speak until he made eye contact with me. "You were wrong, love. So wrong. It was very much my fucking problem, because you're mine. Coming to me with the issue wouldn't have hurt me, but keeping it from me does. You don't have to put yourself through hell out of some warped sense of reparation. That isn't how life works."

"All I do is hurt you—even when I try not to. You should let me go. You deserve so much better than me." He pulled free from my grasp and chewed on his thumbnail. "You don't owe me your blind loyalty just because you love me. I'm bad for you, Max."

This was worse than I ever thought it could be. My love sat before me broken and in pain, and he didn't think he was worthy of better. "Listen to me carefully," I said in a stern tone that caught his attention. "My devotion to you isn't blind. I see that you're not perfect, and I want you regardless. I see your flaws and your pain, and I still want you—I'm still choosing you." I ducked my head for a moment, looking for the resolve to say everything I needed to. "We're all looking for somebody to love, and I've found you. You're it for me, Rem, and that's not a compromise on my part.

"I won't force you to stay if you truly want to leave, but if you think you have to, I'm telling you, you don't. I want you here with me more than anything, and today hasn't changed that in the slightest. I need you to understand that. So I'm asking you again to please, please stay with me."

Remy wasn't moving. He might have even been holding his breath before his chest heaved on a long exhale. "I don't want to keep hurting you. I feel like I'm falling, and I don't know how to stop."

"Fall on me. Stay with me. Promise me you'll talk to me

about anything. I can handle whatever you're going through, but I need to know about it."

Remy dragged his teeth across his bottom lip, then sighed, looking even more drained than he had in the shower. "Will you do the same?"

My brows flew up at his redirect. After what I'd just asked of him, I couldn't lie or downplay my own issues without being the world's biggest hypocrite. Talking about the extent of how much my scar bothered me wouldn't be easy, but I was asking a lot of Remy, and that couldn't be easy on him either. It was a fair request, so I nodded.

"Can you say it, please?"

"I promise I'll be completely honest about everything." I swallowed hard. "Including my revulsion to my scar and how much it controls me sometimes."

Remy bowed his head and cleared his throat. "We're a fuckin' mess, you and I. Me more so than you." He smiled, though it was shaky and didn't reach his eyes.

"I want you as you are, Rem. If you're broken now, I want to be there to help you heal."

"Okay. I'm so fucking sorry. The words are probably worthless right now, but I mean them." He still looked so lost and unsure despite my promise.

"Come here," I said, patting my leg. He climbed into my lap without hesitation. "I'm sorry that you had to go through this alone." I ghosted my finger over where he'd been struck earlier. "Are you okay?"

He shrugged. "I've been hit harder than that before."

"Remy," I chided.

"That wasn't funny. I'm sorry. I'm… I don't know. I really don't know."

"That's all right." I kissed his cheek, then his forehead. "Is there anything else I should know before we put today behind us?"

Remy's eyes darkened and he looked frightened. "I—"

He cut himself off and looked away. I caught his chin between my thumb and index finger and turned him back toward me. My lips met his in a slow press, then he whimpered and melted against me. The nagging uncertainty that'd plagued me since we got home melted away, and I felt like I had him back.

"I mean it—you can tell me anything."

"You're not gonna like it." I kissed him again to dispel his doubts. "I was planning on killing myself—back in Cali."

My mouth fell open, and I clutched him tighter. "*What?*"

His mouth trembled, but he pressed on. "I was going to do it that night the hospital called me. I don't know exactly why I even answered the phone. I was at my lowest point, and I didn't have a reason to keep going."

"You have me, and Rosalind."

He shook his head. "I didn't then. I was going to do it after your shoulder got better—after I had a chance to try to make amends. Then you asked me to stay, and I wanted to. Somewhere along the way I realized that I couldn't fucking go through with it." He hid his face in my neck and inhaled deeply. "You smell like home, Max. Like everything I've always wanted and didn't deserve." He pulled back and brushed his thumb over my lips, catching my scar. "I love you more than I could ever say."

"I love you too." I kissed him again, only to be interrupted by his yawn.

"I'm sorry. Long fucking day."

I nodded, then let go of him. "We could both use some rest."

He grunted, stealing a page out of my book, then rolled out of my lap. He was only gone long enough for me to lie down, and then he was back, resting his head on my chest.

"You swore today, babe."

I hummed, twirling my fingers around his nape.

"You swore twice."

"It's not going to happen again. And don't tell Macalister."

He groaned. "*Fuck.* That guy is going to hate me again."

"He won't. I'll talk to him."

"No, I think I should. How did you find me, anyway?" he asked, craning his neck to look at me.

"Your laptop. I—" I stumbled over the words, suddenly embarrassed. "I guessed your password and checked your messages to find out where you'd gone."

Remy kissed my chest, then set his head back down. "Thank you. I have to give that money back."

"No more of that tonight. We can talk about it after we've gotten some sleep. We'll get it sorted."

"Okay."

Within minutes, Remy's breathing evened out and he fell asleep. Today was a righteous mess, but I had hope that we'd go into tomorrow with more perspective and we'd fix it. *We* weren't broken—everything else could be worked on with time.

EIGHTEEN

REMY

I'D BEEN SUCH A FUCKING idiot about nearly everything in my life. I'd lied, cheated, abandoned those who loved me, lived a soulless, vapid life, and yet I'd still been given another chance. I woke up plastered against Maxim's side with a leg over one of his, and his arm around me. Despite how awful the last twenty hours had been, I felt safe.

Even so, I was still a massive idiot. I thought I'd lost everything, but I still had Max. For whatever reason, I still had Max, and my stupidity had almost cost me him. I'd meant it when I promised him I'd be honest about everything from here on. I wouldn't make the same mistakes that kept me feeling miserable. It was going to be an adjustment, but I'd fucking do it for him—maybe even for myself one day.

If I thought I didn't deserve Maxim before, I sure as hell didn't now. I also knew that I couldn't live without him, and I didn't have to. Whether I thought I deserved him or not didn't change my feelings for him, or his for me. It took me a long time to understand that, and would likely be something I'd be reminding myself of daily. I had to trust that Maxim could love me while looking out for himself. I still believed that I'd be his downfall, but I couldn't expect those feelings to change after one fucking nap.

Regret would be with me for a long time as well. My desperation-fueled horrible decision and the shame I'd felt when Maxim saw me on my knees are things that would undoubtedly stay with me. I tipped my head up to see his face, or at least part of it, and was startled to see his head propped up and his eyes open.

"Did I wake you up?" I asked in a rough voice.

A subtle shake of his head answered my question. "I've been awake for about an hour."

"Yeah?"

"I've been thinking. How much money did that email say you owed?"

The reality of yesterday came crashing back, souring what should have been another lazy, sex-filled morning with Maxim. "Just under ten grand."

He hummed, drawing his brows together in thought. He kissed my forehead, then moved to sit up, stopped by my tightened grip.

"Where are you going?"

"I have to tell Rosalind you're okay. And I'd like to have my lawyer take a look at that email. We'll pay whatever is legally owed."

I sighed, rolling onto my back. "You mean you will." I sounded like a brat—I knew I did. I just hated feeling like I was taking advantage of Maxim.

"Rem," he said, sounding as exhausted as I felt, yet somehow still sympathetic. "It's not the same. It's not, okay?" He ran his hand over the hair obscuring my forehead, letting the strands slip between his fingers. "I'm going to help you because I love you and I want to. I would do the same thing for Macalister or Bryan if they needed it."

"It's a lot of money for you."

"I wouldn't toss you aside, regardless of how much was on the line. All I want is for you to be happy and safe. Ten thousand dollars isn't a lot to pay for that."

"Promise me you'll let me pay you back when my trust is released." I still had three years left of the funds being held hostage by my parents. After that, they could fuck off.

He nodded. "If that's what you need. I'll be right back." Maxim rose to his feet and the sight of him naked was almost enough to make me forget about the mess I'd dragged him into.

No, that wasn't right. He'd willingly entered into it, and I had to recognize that there was a difference. This wasn't me bringing Maxim down; this was him choosing to help me, and I had to respect his decision.

"I'm sorry. I know you don't like it when I talk shit about myself, but this is hard for me."

"It's all right. This adjustment will take time. We've both been less forthcoming than we should have been. All we can do now is work at improving that going forward." He slipped on a pair of boxers, which did very little to diminish any distraction. "Are you hungry?"

"Yeah."

"I'll bring some breakfast after I make a few calls. Do you…" He bit his lip and lowered his gaze from mine. "Do you mind if I use your computer? I might need to forward that email."

"Go ahead." I propped myself up on my elbows while he picked up my MacBook, which was still on the floor from when he'd used it yesterday—or however many hours ago it was. "I'm not pissed about what you did. I mean it. You don't have to feel guilty. I don't want to think about where I'd be if you hadn't."

Maxim clenched a fist by his side and inhaled sharply,

clearly displeased by the mention of how he'd found me. "You don't have to worry about that now. Rest. I'll be back."

I tracked his movements as he left the room, then fell flat on my back. Maxim's voice floated in from the living room, but I drifted off before I could discern who he was talking to.

WHEN I WOKE up again it was clearly night. No cracks of light peeked around the edges of the curtains, and the city was quieter than it would be during the morning or afternoon. The bed felt too damn good, though my full bladder and growling stomach had other plans.

I rolled out of bed and slipped on some pajamas pants before heading for the bathroom. Once I was back in the hall, the distinct smell of pizza filled my nose and made my stomach growl again.

Max was in the kitchen, chopping up an orange bell pepper and keeping an eye on a pan on the stove. His lips lifted in that adorable lopsided grin when he saw me.

"Hi," he said, almost sounding shy.

"Hey." I leaned against the counter on the other side of the stove with my arms crossed. "You didn't wake me up."

"I tried. You were sound asleep. I figured you needed it."

That was fair. "What time is it?"

"Almost eight. There's pizza in the oven, and I'm also making some rice so it'll be perfect for frying tomorrow."

"Fuck, you're perfect. And here I thought you were going to make me eat vegetables," I replied, rubbing my stomach.

Maxim hummed, then set down the knife and opened the fridge. He pulled out a bowl of mixed greens, tomatoes, sliced cukes, and some small cubes of feta—a fucking salad. "I forgot to add peppers earlier. You're not having any pizza until you eat at least half of this."

"It's like that now?"

He tried to hide a smirk as he bowed his head and grunted.

"What kind of pizza is it?"

"Lou Malnati's. Pepperoni and double sausage," he answered in a smug tone. That handsome bastard knew I wouldn't be able to say no to that.

"*Shit*," I hissed. "I accept your terms."

He hummed again, not looking up from his task. A silence I wasn't too comfortable with fell over us, and I didn't know how to feel about it. I was more than used to silence with Maxim, but this felt almost awkward. It wasn't him— he'd treated me with nothing but love and understanding. It was me; I couldn't shake how guilty I felt about how I'd handled my situation.

Before I could get too deep into my self-loathing, Maxim wrapped his arms around me and pulled me snug against him. The fingers of one hand teased my nape while his other clutched my waist. "Stay with me, love."

They were the same words he'd said to me before, though they had a double meaning now. I returned his embrace and closed my eyes, breathing in his familiar scent mixed with the aromas from his cooking. Maxim was a solid reminder of why moving past this was so important. Dwelling on my shitty choices wouldn't do either of us any good. I had to try harder and do everything I could.

"I think I need to see a shrink."

Maxim rubbed up the side of my neck, just behind my ear. "I think that would be wise. Maybe... I should too."

"Yeah? Okay." I huffed out a deep breath, feeling lighter.

"In the spirit of transparency, I have a few things to tell you. They can wait until after we eat, though."

I pulled back far enough to look up at Maxim and raised a brow. "You can't drop that and not tell me right away."

"They're good things… I think."

I narrowed my eyes at him and growled, though it didn't sound nearly as sexy as when he did it.

"Braddock officially offered me a new job as a superintendent, and I said yes."

My eyes went so wide they nearly popped out of my skull, and my smile was just as big. "Holy shit—are you serious?"

He nodded and grunted quietly. "It will be an adjustment, but I think it will work. I'll be in charge, though not in everyone's focus."

I lifted up on my toes to press my lips to his when I felt his hands slid down under my ass and lift me up. I gasped as our lips met and he spun us around to set me on the clean part of the counter.

"I'm so fucking proud of you. You're going to be perfect."

"Thank you. It has a fairly significant pay increase as well, which brings me to my second point." He looked down and licked his lips, clearly nervous. "I've been speaking to my financial advisor about buying a house. I've even gone to some open houses over the last couple of months." Maxim rubbed his hands up and down my spread thighs, giving them a light squeeze near the top. "I was thinking of surprising you, but I should have spoken to you about it. So, I'm asking now: do you want to live with me? In a proper home of our own?"

I stared at him blankly with my mouth ajar while I processed his words. There were a hundred reasons why I felt I should say no: self-doubt, me being underserving, and taking advantage of Maxim being near the top. Though they were drowned out by my overwhelming desire to be close to him. I loved him with every fiber of my fucking soul, and I wanted to believe that we could be happy again.

"Remy?"

"Yes." I cupped his neck, lacing my fingers together at his nape and nodded enthusiastically. "Fuck yes, Max."

His eyes lit up before he closed the short distance between us and kissed me so tenderly that I forgot all about my hunger. I hooked my ankles behind him, keeping him close while I deepened the kiss with a sweep of my tongue against his.

A loud beep made both of us jump and break apart. "The pizza is ready," Maxim said, his chest heaving.

"I'm not hungry anymore." It was then that my stomach betrayed my words with the loudest groan of protest. I squeezed my eyes shut and muttered a curse while Maxim broke into a rich, deep laugh.

He gave my sore cheek a soft peck, then stepped back and slipped on an oven mitt. "You're a bad liar."

"That one doesn't really count."

Maxim shook his head, then opened the oven and took out the pizza, setting the pan on the unused back burners.

I slid off the counter, resigned to the idea of eating the best pizza in the world. "Did you go out and get this while I was asleep?"

"Macalister brought it over. He called earlier to check in." He handed me two plates, then the bowl of salad. I had to admit that it looked pretty good.

A sigh forced its way out of me, though it wasn't one of defeat. I really had to thank that guy later.

"Go on. Let's eat."

With one last quick peck, I headed for the living room with Maxim right behind me.

KEEPING up with the trend of not putting off difficult conversations and being open, we discussed Maxim's call to his lawyer after supper. It was advised we pay back the cost of the flight and the money I'd spent upon arriving back in Chicago. All else was Stan being petty and vindictive. *Shocker.*

Maxim's lawyer drafted up a reply on the office letterhead basically saying we were ready for court and looking forward to explaining the nature of our relationship to a judge. Maxim had wanted my approval before giving the go-ahead for the response to be sent. I gladly gave it. Stan cared too much about his public image to be dragged in open court, no matter how angry he was with me. Maybe I'd have been able to come to that conclusion myself had I not panicked when I got his message.

I returned the money from the "party" and blocked Jonas's number. Maxim wanted to strangle the life out of him, though he seemed content enough with me promising not to contact him again. I thought that was more than fair.

Roz was angry with me when I told her what I'd done. I also had to persuade her not to kill Jonas and stooped as low as reminding her of her Hippocratic oath, which she didn't hesitate correcting me on. Apparently, that was an outdated custom and movies and television were a lie. Go figure.

Maxim and I spent most of the next week at home catching up on his teen dramas. He kept up with his gym routine and I hunted for jobs on the days I didn't go with him. I hadn't yet made a resume, but I'd bookmarked everything that seemed probable. I wouldn't be doing anything glamorous, yet I was sure anything would be better than sitting around alone once Maxim went back to work. Everything was relatively normal aside from the fact that we hadn't had sex since *that* day.

I didn't think it was a lack of attraction; Maxim still looked at me the same as he'd done before, and I definitely still wanted him. For some reason, we just weren't connecting sexually. Everything else was unaffected. We talked more, we laughed, and we spent even more time together. It was almost like neither of us knew what to say to show that that aspect of us was okay. I sure didn't, anyway.

The season three finale of *The Originals* I'd half been paying attention to came to an end, and Maxim shut off the TV. He was being the responsible one and insisting we go to bed at a reasonable time because we were having a couples therapy session tomorrow morning. Begrudgingly, I dragged my ass off of the couch and out of Maxim's embrace.

I finished brushing my teeth first and left him in the bathroom while I crawled into bed. Once I finally got the blankets sorted, I startled when I saw Maxim leaning against the doorframe, watching me. The set of his brow made him look troubled or deep in thought—it was hard to tell in the dimly lit room.

"What's up, babe?" I asked.

He took a deep breath, then walked over to the closet, completely ignoring my question. With deliberate actions, he moved several things aside and pulled out a small box from the top shelf. With his back still to me, he clutched the box tight enough for his forearm muscles to flex.

"Max?" I sat up and swung my legs over the edge of the bed, about to get up and go to him.

"Rem." Something in his voice halted my movements, and I gripped the edge of the mattress. He faced me, then closed the short distance between us with four strides. With the box still clutched in his hand, he sank to his knees in front of me and looked… almost scared.

"What's wrong?" I reached for him, and he caught my hand with his free one, stealing my breath.

Maxim turned my hand, then kissed the inside of my wrist before he released me. I waited with bated breath until his eyes flicked up and met mine; I saw nothing but love in them.

"I'm sorry if I'm acting strange. I… I can't think straight when you touch me sometimes, and this is important."

I dipped my head to let him know I was listening, though I remained silent.

"I won't sugarcoat this; when you left me back then, I thought I was going to die. I honestly didn't how I would go on without you. Time didn't make it hurt any less, nor did it diminish my feelings for you. Now that I know what it feels like to lose you and have you back, I know wholeheartedly that I love you more now than ever before." He held up his hand holding the box, then opened it.

My eyes stung with the warning of tears as I stared down at a ring box. It was the same one I'd seen when Maxim proposed. He opened the box and a cry escaped me when I saw our rings. They were a little tarnished, but just as beautiful as I remembered them.

Maxim picked up the smaller of the two gold bands and swallowed hard. "Will you wear this again, and let everyone know that you're mine? Just as I'll wear the other to show that I'm yours. Remy, will you marry me?"

"Yes," I forced out with trembling hands and a shaky voice. "God, yes, Max. Yes."

He set the box on the bed, then slid the ring—*my ring*—onto my finger. Seeing it there was too much, and I couldn't hold back the tears that fell from my eyes, nor could I stop the sobs that shook my shoulders.

Maxim wiped away my tears with a smile, then I picked up his ring and slipped it onto his ring finger. The sight of it there along with my own caused me to choke up. It was like an invisible force was squeezing my throat, but I craved it. The force of it brought me closer to Maxim and then I was in his warm embrace again.

He kissed me soft and slow, and I devoured him in turn, taking everything I could. His pace matched mine in seconds and I was on my back in the middle of the bed with Maxim's weight pressing on me.

"I need you," I rasped in his ear. I felt lightheaded, whether from the euphoria of having everything I'd always wanted, or all of the blood rushing to my dick, I wasn't sure. It was probably both, but I couldn't think about anything but him.

We tore off each other's clothes like they were ablaze, yet the heat between us only increased with each discarded item. When we were skin-to-skin, the fuzzy feeling in my head had me feeling almost drunk. I clawed at Maxim and touched him everywhere I could, somehow needing to feel him on every inch of me.

In the wake of a bite to my neck hard enough to almost make me come, he pulled back and stretched over me. When he slid back down, he pressed one—no, two—slicked fingers inside me, making me wince, though it quickly turned into a moan when I breathed out. Maxim swallowed up the sound as he locked his mouth to mine, his skilled tongue and fingers working in time to tear me apart.

After one graze over my prostate, Maxim withdrew his fingers, and I mourned the loss of him—only for a moment. The delightful stretch and burn when he entered me had me uttering curses and digging my nails into his back. He rolled his hips in slow, deliberate thrusts that targeted my prostate and had us both coming within minutes.

We were a mess of entwined sweaty limbs when Maxim's cock finally slipped free of me. I was a fuckin' mess, yet neither of us moved until we caught our breath, and even then, it was only so Maxim could flip us over. I lay pressed against his side and spun the gold ring on his finger as he rested his hand on his chest.

"What's on your mind?" he asked in a sleepy, satiated voice.

"Nothing."

"Rem."

"Shit, don't you wanna wait until you find out the extent of my crazy tomorrow?"

He shook his head, determination never wavering. "It doesn't matter. I'm going to love you tomorrow just as much as I do tonight." He brought my fingers to his lips and kissed each of them. "Don't ever doubt my feelings for you."

"I love you, Max—so much that it scares me. I'm not certain about much of anything in my life, but I know with everything I am that I love you. So fucking much."

"I love you too, Rem."

I drifted off while listening to the steady beat of Maxim's heart and rubbing my engagement ring with my thumb. I had a second chance to see my unfulfilled promise through to the end, and I vowed to never break it again. Not just for Maxim's sake, but for my own as well. He'd been right when he'd said that we were all just looking for somebody to love. I could overcomplicate everything as much as I wanted, but his words remained true. We weren't searching anymore, and I wasn't alone; we had each other, and the rest we could figure out in time.

EPILOGUE

MAXIM

Six Months Later

AFTER SPENDING NEARLY eight hours supervising on a worksite near the West Loop, I was back at the office finishing up some paperwork. On days like today when I wanted nothing more than to go home after a long day, I detested my promotion. Days like today were few, though. I was on edge because I hadn't seen Remy in three days.

He'd gone to a music festival with his sister in San Francisco. They'd invited me, but I couldn't leave in the middle of a job. He'd arrived back around noon, then went straight to work, though he should be finishing up soon.

As much as I wished I could have gone with them, I knew getting away would be beneficial for him. Our therapist had stated that it was a good idea for us to have time away from each other occasionally. She said it was paramount that we maintain our separate identities, which I understood.

We typically had one couples session every three weeks, an individual session once a week for Remy, and once every two weeks for me. Remy was still battling with his self-worth and had been diagnosed with clinical depression, though he had fewer dark days. Once the right medication was prescribed, he seemed so much more like his old self.

My own treatment was also making a positive impact on my daily life. When I was diagnosed with body dysmorphic disorder and learned more about it, I felt like a fool for trying to hide that I'd been struggling for so long. Remy had suspected it, but hearing my doctor and therapist explain it to me made me understand that my behavior wasn't normal—I'd just been coping with it since I was a child.

We'd tried cognitive behavioral therapy first due to my reluctance to take antidepressants or any other drugs. Exposure and response prevention in particular seemed to be working best. Remy was amazing in helping me with it. There were times he could identify when I was trying to hide or shift focus away from myself, without me even realizing I was doing it.

I checked the wall clock and rubbed along my clean-shaven jaw—keeping up with shaving had become part of my therapy. If I came in early tomorrow morning to finish these documents, I could catch Remy leaving work if left now.

Without further deliberation, I stacked up the papers strewn about on my desk, locked them in a drawer, then left to catch a cab. I usually took the bus or Metra, but I was in a rush to see my fiancé.

WHEN I WALKED up to the storefront of Eat Cake, the closed sign was flipped yet the door was unlocked. I entered, smiling at the familiar faces inside. Bryan hadn't yet changed into his regular clothes and was wiping down the coffee machine while Elijah and Dubhlainn chatted at a table in the corner.

What had me laughing was seeing Remy in his apron behind the counter, arguing with Macalister. They were both leaning forward, almost touching.

"You're the fuckin' worst. No way is 'Ice Ice Baby' better than 'Under Pressure.' Get the fuck out," Remy hissed.

Macalister threw his head back and barked out a laugh. "Oh, shove it, Gambit. Sucking up to the boss just because he loves Queen isn't going to score you any points."

"Actually, it's going to score him all the points," Bryan said, unbuttoning his white chef coat.

"I'm not saying 'Under Pressure' isn't a great song, because it is. But 'Ice Ice Baby' is *iconic*. It's got more than double the YouTube views—just saying."

Bryan snorted and went back to ignoring them while Remy threw his hands up in frustration. "Since when is fucking YouTube a good measure of anything?"

"Says Mr. Instagram *influencer*," Mac quipped.

Remy growled, looking like he was about to jump the counter and tackle Macalister. I took that as my cue to make my presence known.

I cleared my throat and all eyes landed on me. Instead of trying to make myself as small and inconspicuous as possible, I stood tall and proud with a smile on my face.

"Max," Remy said as he hopped over the counter and bounded toward me.

I caught him in a tight hug and our lips met instantly. We were hungry for each other after the days apart, and the kiss showed it. I heard Macalister shiver and utter "gross," while Bryan and Dubhlainn whistled.

I pulled back first, smoothing his brown hair out of his face. It was dyed back to its natural light brown color now, though he had a similar cut with the sides shaved. "I missed you."

He kissed me again quickly, then spun around. "Am I good to go, Bry?"

Bryan nodded and Remy untied his apron. He took it off, balled it up, then threw it at Macalister's unsuspecting face. I grabbed him by the arm and led him out as Dubhlainn jumped up and held Macalister back as he laughed.

Once outside, we headed down the street and I kept my eyes open for another cab. There was no way I was waiting forty-five minutes to get home via the Green Line or bus.

"You're trouble," I said to Remy as I slipped my arm around his waist.

"He's annoying. He's been calling me Gambit for two weeks straight since I got my haircut."

I bit back a smile and squeezed his hip. "He calls you Gambit not just for your haircut. He likes you." Remy opened his mouth to speak, but I cut him off. "Think about it, Rem. X-Men is his favorite comic series. You two are like kids with platonic schoolyard crushes with all the veiled name-calling and insults. It's pretty adorable."

Remy groaned. "At least it's not Remington Steele anymore."

"Enough of that. Tell me about your trip."

He launched into a play-by-play of the weekend that lasted the entire trip home, and then some. The sun had begun to set by the time I unlocked the door to our Oak Park home. We'd moved in two months ago and still had some rooms to paint and furnishings to update, but it was ours. I locked the door behind us, then pushed Remy against it, forcing the air out of his lungs and cutting off his story about getting recognized from his Instagram days by a pair of teenaged girls.

I crashed my lips to his and felt him melt in my arms. I

slid my hands around the backs of his thighs and lifted him up, giving him the better angle to deepen the kiss. His arms and legs wrapped around me while he worked me over with his tongue and the occasional nip to my scar.

"Welcome home, love."

The lust in his eyes simmered, and he looked into my eyes as a shy smile stretched across his lips. "Welcome home, Max."

We'd taken to that exchange every day since we moved in. Neither of us grew up in loving homes, and it was important to us to cherish what we had now.

We were finally home and together; the rest of the world ceased to matter.

ALSO BY SERENE FRANKLIN

Spread: getbook.at/spread

Turning Out: getbook.at/turningout

Princes of the Universe (Crazy Little Thing Book One):
getbook.at/princes

Killer Queen (Crazy Little Thing Book Two):
getbook.at/killerqueen

ABOUT THE AUTHOR

Serene Franklin lives in Halifax (Nova Scotia, not California), but has fallen in love with Chicago through research and writing. She has a political science degree, and—more importantly—an adorable and mildly irritating Goldendoodle named Tai.

When not writing, she enjoys reading, cooking spicy food, listening to music, losing at crib, and watching anime. Serene is a proud otaku and collector of anime figures in addition to novels and yaoi manga.

Serene currently writes contemporary MM romance, but has plans to branch out into other subgenres.

Email: sfwrites801@gmail.com

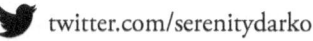 twitter.com/serenitydarko

instagram.com/serenity_darko

bookbub.com/profile/serene-franklin